2020
FRESH CLEAN
JOKES
FOR KIDS

2020 FRESH CLEAN JOKES FOR KIDS

Written & illustrated by

V. SUBHASH

2020 Fresh Clean Jokes For Kids

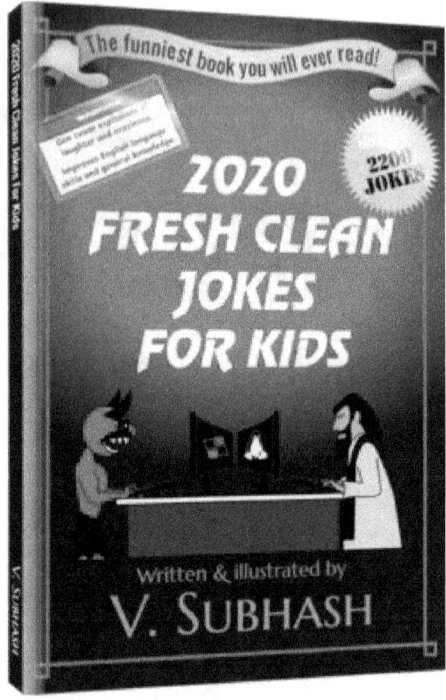

Written, illustrated and designed by

V. Subhash
(www.VSubhash.in)

Copyright

First edition

Published in 2020 by V. Subhash.

Preface

When I was a kid, I read an American jokebook and here is the result. (I should have read Shakespeare instead.) Initially, it was a mystery to me as to what the fuss was in crossing a road. The book was nevertheless funny and I enjoyed reading it. This 2020 jokebook is based on that model.

I have included many jokes in this book to make the reader become familiar with new words and facts. This book is a good choice for children who wish to improve their English-language skills and general knowledge. It will secretly kindle their curiosity and encourage them to learn new things. Specifically, it has answers to many of the amusing riddles and questions that kids are asked in schools by their teachers and friends. Many jokes in this book use misleading information in mock seriousness. While most teenagers should be able to easily identify them, younger kids will need guidance. Kids should be encouraged to use a dictionary, an atlas and an encylopedia to cross-reference unfamiliar information. If the kid does not have these books, then do not suggest the Internet or a computer as an alternative. Do not interrupt a kid's reading with computers or other electronic devices.

V. Subhash
20-02-2020

Contents

- **Part 1 – For Learning**
  This part of the book is written to improve general knowledge and English vocabulary.
  - Children's Jokes [8]
  - Computer Jokes [13]
  - Computer Programming Jokes [18]
  - Cross-The-Road Jokes [23]
  - Elephant And Ant Jokes [28]
  - Animal Jokes [33]
  - Fancy Creature Jokes [51]
  - Geography Jokes [55]
  - Jokes You Love To Hate [63]
  - Knock-Knock Jokes [84]
  - Mix Jokes [89]
  - Physics Jokes [91]
  - Chemistry Jokes [94]
  - Biology Jokes [100]
  - Medical Jokes [107]
  - Pun Jokes [112]
  - Useful French Phrases [122]
  - Useful Latin Phrases [125]
  - Other Useful Foreign Phrases [128]
- **Part 2 – For Fun**
  This part is purely for the hedonistic consumption of humour.
  - Financial Jokes [131]
  - Jokes In Advertising [133]
  - Off-The-Wall Philosophers [138]
  - Political Jokes [145]
  - Rajinikanth Facts [151]
  - Breakup Jokes [153]

Part 1 - For Learning

This part of the book is written to improve English vocabulary and general knowledge.

Children's Jokes

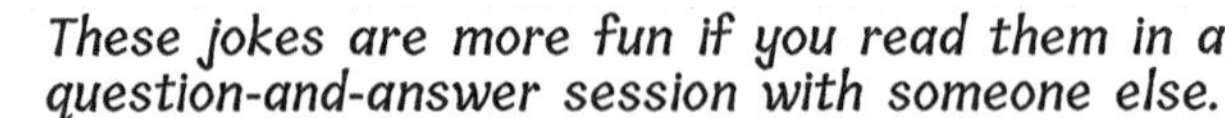

These jokes are more fun if you read them in a question-and-answer session with someone else.

- **What do hummingbirds like to read?**
  Musical notes.

- **Why did the chicken cross the road?**
  It saw a *zebra crossing*.

In some countries, a 'road crossing' or 'crosswalk' is known as a *zebra crossing*.

- **Why did the zebra cross the road?**
  The chicken dared it.

- **Which came first? The chicken or the egg?**
  - The chicken. It had legs and won the race.
  - Which chicken? Which egg?

- **What did the rolodex say to the calendar?**
  "Your *days are numbered*."

- **What did the calendar say to the rolodex?**
  "You may have many friends but I get a lot of holidays."

- **What did the new calendar say to the old calendar?**
  "Your days are over, buddy!"

- **Why did the pencil not like the eraser?**
  It *rubs both ways*.

- **Why does the cow go moo?**
  It does not. It says, "Maaaaah". And, the sheep does not go "Baa". It goes, "Meheheheh!"

- **What kind of cheese talks?**
  Say Cheese!

- **What did the wall clock say?**
  "My time is up!"

- **Why did the lizard sue the hospital?**
  After it broke off its tail, a psychiatrist wanted to treat it as a split-personality disorder.

Autotomy is the ability in some animals with which they can break off a body part to distract or escape from a predator. The shed body part usually regenerates.

- **How does a horse fly?**
  Horse feathers!

- **Which one of these is not a duck – Bombay Duck, Mandarin Duck, Muscovy Duck and Swedish Duck?**
  Hint: It is a fish, usually consumed in dried form.

- **Which one of these is not a fish – Bluefish, Goldfish, Redfish and Silverfish?**
  Hint: It is a wingless insect usually found in old books or clothing.

- **How did the goose get run over by a car?**

It didn't *take a gander.*

- ## How does a fish go to war?
  In a tank.

- ## Is half a glass half-empty or half-full?
  This is an urban legend that originated as a joke in the TV sitcom *The Lucy Show* and has captured the imagination of generations of psychologists and interviewers. Anyone, who thinks that only an optimist will consider half a glass as half-full, has low standards. Someone, who thinks only a pessimist will consider it as half-empty, has no standards.

- ## The word *suffrage* refers to voting rights. Did it originally involve any suffering?
  No, the word is derived from the Medieval Latin *suffragium*, which refers to a voting ballot/tablet, the right to vote or simply the vote. The anglicized version *suffrage* began to be used in the 18th century.

- ## What is the opposite of the adjective *hungry*?
  There is no direct opposite such as *unhungry* or *nonhungry* but *satiated* seems to be all right.

I found this question in my sibling's English reader. I did not know the answer. Neither did several other people to whom I posed the

- ## Can you say 100 words in one minute? None of the words should have the letters A, B, C or D.

  Zero, one, two, three, four... ninety-nine.

- ## Complete the word ladder – From DULL to MOOD

  One and only one letter can change in each rung of the ladder. No acronyms, proper nouns or loan words.

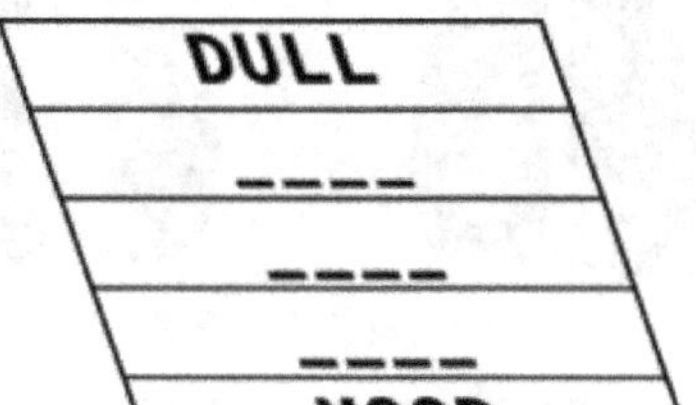

- ## Phantom Hand Challenge

  This is a prank you can play on others. Ask one of them to hold out their arm as shown in this illustration. Place your index and middle finger on the person's wrist and slowly walk them towards the elbow pit. After you start, tell the person to close his/her eyes and open it only when your fingers reach the elbow pit. No matter how many times this is done, the person's brain will always be prematurely tricked into thinking that your fingers has reached the pit.

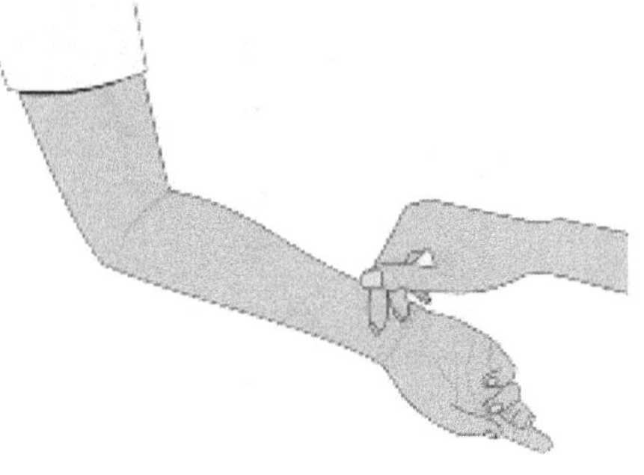

- ## What's the difference between these animals: elk, moose, reindeer and caribou?

  The moose (*Alces alces*) is the most funny-looking one and is found in sub-Arctic regions of North America and Eurasia. Parts of their antlers appear flattened. They are usually solitary animals.

  The elk (*Cervus canadensis*) is smaller than the moose but bigger than the reindeer.

Elks are found in USA, Canada, eastern Russia, north-eastern China and Mongolia. In many parts of Europe, the elk is confusingly referred as a moose.

Reindeer and caribou are the same species of *Rangifer tarandus*. They are found mostly in Arctic regions of Canada, Alaska and Eurasia. The reindeer and elk look similar but you can tell the difference by their footprint. They do not have flat antlers like the moose. Reindeer is the only deer species where both the male and female have antlers.

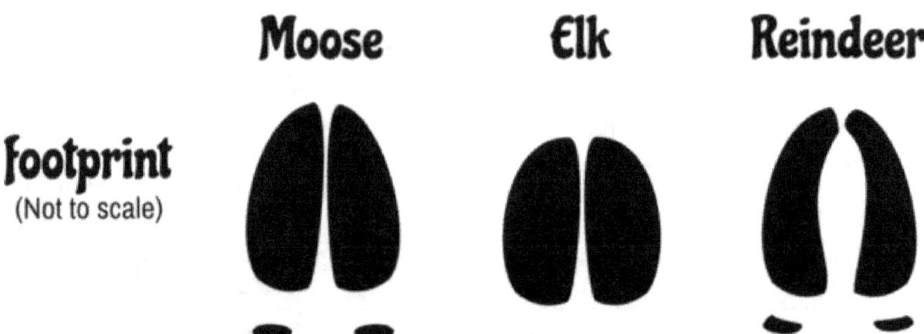

- **Complete the word ladder – from FUNNY to JOKES**

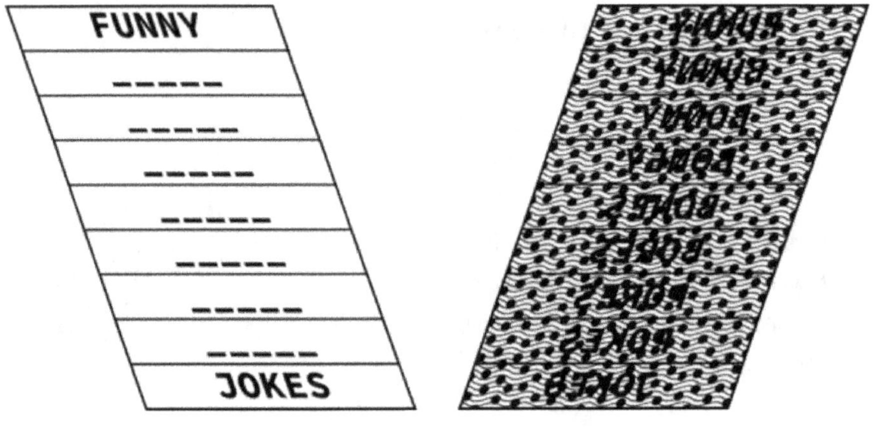

One and only one letter can change in each rung of the ladder. No acronyms, proper nouns or non-English (loan) words.

Computer Jokes

Do you use computers? If not, start with a Linux computer and you will be a cut above the rest. Linux is a free and open-source software (FOSS) operating system (OS). If you already have a computer, install Linux as a virtual machine (VM) and see if you like it. Linux has FOSS alternatives for most proprietary software that you use. All the illustrations in this book were created using Inkscape and GIMP. Both are FOSS and available for other operating systems too.

- What happened after the robot's 3D printer broke?
  No arm done.

- What made the quantum computer so frustrated?

He made *a complete fool of himself*.

- **What did one byte say to another?**
  A bit of advice.

- **Why did exclamation mark key (!) break up with the question mark key (?)?**
  There was *a question about* his character.

- **What did dollar key ($) say to the Euro key (€) about the pound key (#)?**
  That he is of *Sterling (£) character*.

- **Why did the dot key feel down?**
  o Its character was called into question (?).
  o A question mark was hanging over it.

- **Why was the space key depressed?**
  It had no character.

- **What did one emoji (☺) say to another?**
  "You think I am funny?"

- **What did one emoticon (😀) say to another?**
  "What's with the funny expression?"

- **Why did one emoticon (👎) not like the other?**
  He *stuck out like a sore thumb* .

- **What is your mother's password?**
  Mum's the word.

- **Name the font with no sense of humour?**
  Comic Sans.

- **What style of font does *Fortune* magazine use?**
  Fortune favours the **bold**.

- **If a politician wanted to work in the IT industry, what job designation would he get?**
  Headless server.

- **If a cow wanted to work in the IT industry, where could it go?**
  A server farm.

- **What happened when Unix dæmons attacked Chuck Norris?**
  He hit them so hard they remained misspelled to this day.

- **What happened after Unix dæmons met Rajinikanth?**
  Before meeting him, they were like other processes. Now, they run in the background like zombies.

- **Whois**

  Knock knock
  Who is there?
  man
  Man who?

        man whois

- **Whois**

      Knock knock
      Who is there?
      43
      43 who?
      43 whois

- **Why does espeak have an Italian accent?**
  It converts everything to Roman.

- **What did one network node say to another?**
  "Sorry, I can't talk to you. We are not on the same subnet."

- **How does Count Dracula remain discreet in this networked world?**
  IP cloaking.

- **How do bears find each other in the woods?**
  Bear-to-bear networking.

- **What did one packet say to another?**
  "You are lost, aren't you?"

- **What did the other packet say?**
  "Stop broadcasting it."

- **Why did the security expert couple break up?**
  They routinely probed each other's devices and locked each other out.

- **Why did the hacker couple break up?**
  There were no secrets between them.

- **Why did the hacker couple make up?**
  There were no secrets between them.

- **Why did the backup expert couple break up?**
  They felt they frequently *ran out of* space for each other.

- **Why did the database admin couple break up?**
  Their marriage had reached a deadlock.

- **Why did the network admin couple break up?**
  She thought he was acting like her domain controller.

- **The good, the bad, and the ugly**

      Google: Type your search here.
      Bing: Search me!
      DuckDuckGo: Do you feel lucky... punks?

- **How many Microsoft managers would it take to a change a lightbulb?**
  None but they will trick the bulb to upgrade itself.

- **How many Apple fanboys would it take to a change a lightbulb?**
  One but he would have to buy an Apple-proprietary socket too.

- **How many Apple fanboys would it take to a change a lightbulb?**
  None because Apple has just reinvented the light bulb and a new magical non-revolutionary version is available.

- **Linux or Windows: Who is well-mannered?**
  Lee knocks. Win dozes.

- **Linux vs Windows: Who wins?**
  Lee knocks windoses.

- **What does a server admin think when he looks at his house and vehicle?**
  "That's hardware."

- **What does a server admin think when he thinks of his wife?**
  "That's software."

- **What does a server admin think when he looks at his parents?**
  "My rootware!"

- **What does a server admin think when he looks at his parents-in-law?**
  "Beware!"

- **What does a server admin think when he looks at his kids?**
  "That's malware."

- **What does a server admin think when he looks at his taxes?**
  "That's ransomware."

- **What does a server admin think when he looks at his salary after taxes?**
  "That's shrinkware."

- **What does a server admin think when he notices ants in the server room?**
  "That's social engineering."

- **What does a server admin think when he notices rats in the server room?**
  "Some IP tunnelling."

- **What does a server admin think when he looks at a waiter?**
  "Should I call him a server?"

- **What does a server admin think when he looks at a see-saw?**
  "Seems like a load balancer."

- **What does a server admin think when he looks at a painter?**
  "Hey, an application server."

- **Viral Videos**

  "Our client wants us to log into YouTube and make their corporate videos viral."
  "You want me to sneeze on them?"
  "No, seriously..."
  "I can't catch flu or coronavirus for that!"

- **Stress test - Calculate infinity**

  Linux: Let me get back to you.
  Mac: Look how shiny everything looks.
  Windows: Press Ctrl+Alt+Del to restart.

- **What computer games do Linux enthusiasts like to play?**

  - Command & Conquer
  - Console games

- **What computer game do molemen like to play?**
  Minecraft.

- **What computer game do thieves like to play?**
  Tekken.

- **What computer game do vampires like to play?**
  - Modern Combat
  - Flight Simulator
  - Tomb Raider

- **What computer game do werewolves like to play?**
  Pac-Man.

- **What computer game do zombies like to play?**
  - Half-Life, Left4Dead, Burnout, Dead Rising...
  - Need For Speed, Asphalt, Road Rash
  - Uncharted

- **The Selfie Anthem**

  Jack and Jill
  Livestreamed from a cliff
  When they wanted to take a selfie
  Jack fell down
  And took Jill down
  But the 'likes' were getting silly

• Set to the tune of 'Jack and Jill'.
• Be aware of your surroundings. Life is more important than likes.

Computer Programming Jokes

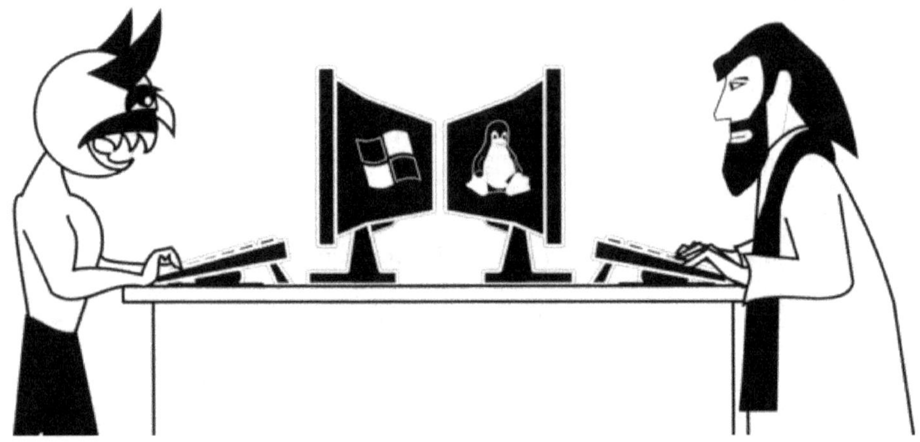

Can you write code? I have written in more than a dozen computer languages, even assembly. How many do you know? This book was written in Markdown using an Eclipse IDE, exported to HTML and formatted using CSS. The jokes were counted using Javascript. Eclipse and many other free software are brought to you by open-source projects.

If you use open-source software, it is expected that you support them financially in the form of donations.

- **What would Jesus do? Choose Linux or Mac or Windows?**
  Linux, of course. This is not a joke!

- **Jesus versus the Devil**
  The Devil challenges Jesus to a computer programming contest. Both start writing the code for their program furiously when suddenly there is a power failure. Both computers go down. When the power comes back, both participants restart their computers. Jesus resumes typing his program without much delay. Meanwhile, the Devil is cooling his heels because Microsoft Windows OS has chosen just that moment to install updates and delayed the login screen. The Devil goes over to the other side and looks at Jesus' computer. Jesus is running a free Linux OS computer, which lets you login immediately. The Devil slaps its forehead and returns to its computer. Windows takes a few more minutes installing updates and finally lets the Devil log in. The Devil opens the IDE and looks at its program. All source code has vanished. The power failure has nuked its file. The Devil again goes over to the other side and wonders, "How come His code is still there?" Then, the Devil remembers, JESUS SAVES.

- **Jesus versus the Devil - Part Deux**
  The Devil challenges Jesus to another challenge. This time, the Devil has a Linux computer and an UPS to handle power failures. Suddenly, the power goes out. The Devil expects Jesus' computer to go down but both computers stay on. The Devil's thoughts are like, "Omigod! What in good heavens is going on?" It goes over to God's computer and finds that the computer is on even though it not connected to any form of emergency power supply. Then, the Devil realizes another truth - GOD WORKS IN MYSTERIOUS WAYS.

- **Code Complete**
  In the book *Code Complete* (Microsoft Press), the author used a neat psychological trick. He listed of a few programming concepts and asked the reader to identify the ones that were familiar. I picked several of those terms and resumed reading what was really a lesson in intellectual honesty. In the list, the author had included a few terms that seemed real but did not really exist. I fell right into his trap and picked a few of the non-existing concepts that I thought I knew. The lesson learned was either you know or you do not. Err on the side of caution.

- **Why did the software routine cry?**
  This method has been deprecated.

- **What did the exception say to the method?**
  "Been there and done that."

- **Why did the base class go to a psychiatrist?**
  It had multiple personality disorder.

- **What did the compiler say to the parser?**
  "Is it just me or *am I seeing double*?"

- **What did the artificial neural network say to the AI program?**
  "You are *getting on my nerves*!"

- **Why did the camel stop speaking to the llama?**
  The llama spoke in ALL CAPS, instead of Camel Case.

- **What did the switch statement say to the computer programmer?**
  "Give me a break!"

- **Why did the switch statement behave erratically?**
  It forgot to take enough breaks.

- **What did the function say to the recursion?**
  "Hold my calls."

- **What charge did the policeman bring against iteration?**
  Nothing except that he is a *repeat offender*.

- **A recursion walks into a bar**
  A recursion walks into a bar and orders tequila shots. The barman pours the drinks but warns, "Don't blow your stack. Okay?"

- **A recursion walks into a bar**
  A recursion walks into a bar and orders a drink. It drinks and then freezes. The bartender walks by and says, "Lost in yourself, eh?"

- **Divide by Zero**

  > Knock! Knock!
  > Who is there?
  > Divide.
  > Divide who?
  > Divide by Zero.
  > Okay, I will *make an exception* for you.

- **Billy, the goat**

  > Knock! Knock!
  > Who is there?
  > Billy.
  > Billy who?
  > Billy, the goat.
  > Sorry, can't let you in. *Gotos are considered evil.*

- **Why did the goat cross the road?**
  To prove that gotos are not evil.

- **Why were the two bytes upset with each other?**
  One of them wanted the other to *move a bit*.

- **How do you prove that a programmer is not crazy?**
  If there is *a method to his madness*.

- **How did the female spider put an end to the male spider stalking her?**
  It used a "nofollow" meta tag.

- **What does the epitaph say for a C programmer?**
  malloc('dd/mm/yyyy');
  free('dd/mm/yyyy');

- **What does the epitaph say for a Java programmer?**
  Nothing. Java variables are automatically garbage-collected.

- **A new software library walks into a bar**
  A new software library walks into a bar and the bartender says, "I would like to see some kind of documentation."

- **Why was the source code angry with the computer programmer?**
  o It did not like his comments.
  o No comments.

- **What would happen if a dog was elected mayor?**
  It would be illegal for software developers to *eat their own dog food*.

This is a metaphor for testing the product before selling it on the market.

- **Why did the tester couple break up?**
  Too many pending issues. Other than logging each other's faults in Bugzilla, no action was taken. Many bugs were labelled as

features and closed without getting fixed.

- **Why did the HTML couple break up?**
  She was strict.
- **Why did the XHTML couple break up?**
  She was very strict.
- **Why did the Unicode couple break up?**
  - He was a reserved character.
  - They were not on the same codepage.
- **What is the source code for the smallest "Hello, World!" executable?**
  This StackOverFlow question was for Windows. The question was locked for deletion ("not a real programming question") before I could answer it. There are three types of executables in Windows - BAT (batch), COM and EXE. Batch files are plain text executables so there is no challenge in it. That leaves us with COM and EXE, which can be created using advanced programming languages. However, all advanced programming languages create very big EXE files... even if you use assembly language. The only solution is to create a COM executable using a DEBUG assembler script. (Uber programmers like us like to etch our code on the bare metal.) Here is the source:

```
a 100
MOV AH,9
MOV DX,108
INT 21
RET
DB "Hello World$"

r CX
14
n hello.com
w
q
```

Put this in a text file named script.txt. Use Command Prompt and redirect the text file to debug.exe. (*debug.exe is available in all old versions of Windows.)

```
debug < script.txt
```

This will create a 20-byte COM executable named hello.com. Execute it by typing *hello*.

```
hello
```

By tradition, the correct text to display is "Hello, World!" with a comma and an exclamation mark. I decided *stick to the letter*.

Code explanation: *A 100* moves to code position 100. You then set 9 to AH register because that is the instruction for interrupt 21 to print a string. Next, you specify the position of the string (required by interrupt 21) in the DX register. This position will be known to you after you finish the RET statement. (You need to

dry run the code interactively once (without the command prompt
redirection) to observe it.) The RET statement returns the
program to the shell. *r CX* is used to specify the number of bytes
of the program - 20 (or 14 in hexadecimal). (This will also be
known during the dry run.) *n* specifies the file name. *w* writes
the file. *q* quits debug.

I got my introduction to debug scripts when reading the Kris Jamsa book
1001 DOS & PC Tips.

- **Two numbers walk in to a bar**
  Two numbers walk in to a bar. One is let in and the other gets
  thrown out. The latter was a *floating-point number*.

- **Two numbers walk in to a bar**
  Two numbers walk in to a bar and have drinks. After a while, one
  of them says it is time to go. He was seeing everything in
  double.

- **How did the DBA couple break up?**
  She felt that in this new UPDATE to her life, she will make a
  better SELECTion who will NOT try to ORDER her or ALTER her.

Cross-The-Road Jokes

Almost everyone has heard the age-old question "Why did the chicken cross the road?" There have been many answers but none were satisfactory. This book settled the debate once for all in the section Children's Jokes. Here is more such jokes.

- **Why did the alien cross the road?**
  It might be a giant leap for man but a small step for a creature from outer space.
- **Why did the postman cross the road?**
  He wanted to get his message across.
- **Why did the drunk cross the road?**
  He was on a roll.
- **Why did the aardvark cross the road?**
  Read the next joke.

An aardvark mainly feeds on ants and termites.

- **Why did the ant cross the road?**
  The ant wanted to make the elephant wait for him by holding up the traffic.

The backgrounder for this joke is available in the section   *Elephant And Ant Jokes* .

- **Why did the badger cross the road?**
  o Everyone was badgering him to do it.
  o There were no legal claws preventing it.
- **Why did the bat cross the road?**
  There is no use flapping about in one place.
- **Why did the bear cross the road?**

He said, "Honey, I am coming."

- **Why did the bee cross the road?**
  Seeing is bee-leaving.

- **Why did the beaver cross the road?**
  It was an *eager beaver*.

- **Why did the camel cross the road?**
  It *sticks its neck out* for nobody.

- **Why did the cat cross the road?**
  When the cat's away, the mice will play.

- **Why did the chameleon cross the road?**
  The colour changed.

- **Why did the cheetah cross the road?**
  To ask the policemen hiding behind the tree whether it *broke the speed limit*.

- **Why did the chimp cross the road?**
  That's quite *a head-scratcher*.

- **Why did the chipmunk cross the road?**
  - It *had the cheek* to do it.
  - Does it seem like a nutty idea to you?

- **Why did the cow cross the road?**
  - There were unsubstantiated reports that *the grass was greener on the other side*.
  - Holy cow! It can do anything it pleases. Cross the road, even. [This joke should be read in Snagglepuss style.]

- **Why did the crocodile cross the road?**
  It saw a Discovery Channel 'animal lover' coming towards it!

- **Why did the crow cross the road?**
  - So, it could *crow about it*!
  - That's the way... as the crow flies.

- **Why did the dog cross the road?**
  Now that scientists have figured out why dogs chase vehicles...

- **Why did the deer cross the road?**
  It was *only a buck*.

- **Why did the donkey cross the road?**
  To show that it does not *dig its heels*.

- **Why did the dragon cross the road?**
  Previously, it was standing in a no-smoking area.

- **Why did the duck cross the road?**
  It didn't want to be *a sitting duck*.

- **Why did the elephant cross the road?**
  Someone told it it was *the next big thing*.

- **Why did the emu cross the road?**
  - No need to get all EMUtional about it.
  - To check if it was worth EMUlating.

- **Why did the firefly cross the road?**

There was no *light at the end of the tunnel* .

- **Why did the fish cross the road?**
  - It wanted to cause a tuna of surprise.
  - When asked, it gave *a canned reply.*
  - Somebody tried to *kick the can down the road* !

- **Why did the frog cross the road?**
  It was only a few hops away.

- **Why did the giraffe cross the road?**
  It was *so over it* .

- **Why did the goat cross the road?**
  For a showdown with the *Men Who Stare At Goats* .

- **Why did the young goat cross the road?**
  It was a *new kid on the block* .

- **Why did the hippopotamus cross the road?**
  It found the hype about it amusing!"

- **Why did the horse cross the road?**
  It was just *horsing around.*

- **Why did the hyena cross the road?**
  It was a *laughing hyena.* It wanted to know what the joke was about.

- **What kind of books do hyenas read?**
  Jokebooks.

- **Animal Collectives**
  Nearly two decades ago, a website run by an English grandmother became famous for the wisdom of the ages that she wanted to share with newer generations. Among them was this selection of collectives.
  - A BUSINESS of ferrets.
  - A CONVOCATION of eagles.
  - A GANG of turkeys.
  - A KNOT of toads.
  - A MOB of kangaroos
  - A MURDER of crows.
  - A PANDEMONIUM of parrots.
  - A PARLIAMENT of owls.
  - A PITYING of turtle doves.
  - A PRICKLE of porcupines.
  - An UNKINDNESS of ravens.

- **Why did the jackal cross the road?**
  It was all jacked up and ready to go.

- **Why did the jaguar cross the road?**
  Ask the driver.

- **Why did the junglefowl cross the road?**
  It always ran aFOUL with *the law of the jungle* .

- **Why did the kangaroo cross the road?**
  It was a joey.

- **Why did the llama cross the road?**
  It was only a spitting distance.

- **Why did the mantis cross the road?**
  Pray, tell me.

- **Why did the lion cross the road?**
  Because the buck stops here.

- **Why did the mole cross the road?**
  It struck *a hole in one* .

- **Why did the monkey cross the road?**
  Monkey see, monkey do.

- **Why did the octopus cross the road?**
  - It was a sucker for a challenge.
  - It wanted some hands-on experience.

- **Why did the owl cross the road?**
  How will I know?

- **Why did the porcupine cross the road?**
  It was *a pressing matter*.

- **Why did the quail cross the road?**
  To prove that it wasn't chicken.

- **Why did the raccoon cross the road?**
  A Native American lost his hat and was looking for a replacement.

- **Why did the rhino cross the road?**
  Somebody pressed the horn.

- **Why did the shark cross the road?**
  To grab a bite.

- **Why did the sheep cross the road?**
  One sheep follows another.
- **Why did the first sheep cross the road?**
  It was led by the shepherd.
- **Why did the shepherd cross the road?**
  The grass was greener on the other side.
- **Why did the silverfish cross the road?**
  No need to *throw the book* at him for that.
- **Why did the snail cross the road?**
  Maybe they have a death-wish.

- **Why did the snake cross the road?**
  Somehow the idea crept into its head.
- **Why did the spider cross the road?**
  Its life was *hanging by a thread*.
- **Why did the squirrel cross the road?**
  It was a nut.
- **Why did the Tasmanian devil cross the road?**
  What the devil made him do it?
- **Why did the toad cross the road?**
  When asked, it had no comments TO ADd.
- **Why did the turkey cross the road?**
  Fat chance it would survive the rest of the year than the road.
- **Why did the turtle cross the road?**
  Shell I tell you?
- **Why did the weasel cross the road?**
  - It could not weasel its way out of a dare.
  - It was tired of this nursery rhyme:

    > Up and down the City Road
    > …
    > Pop! goes the weasel.
- **Why did the xoloitzcuintli cross the road?**
  It went back to get his coat.

Xoloitzcuintli is a dog, also known as the *Mexican hairless*.

- **Why did the yak cross the road?**
  His friends were yacking about it all day.
- **Why did the zebra cross the road?**
  Zebra? Crossing?

In some countries, a 'road crossing' or 'crosswalk' is known as a *zebra crossing*.

Elephant And Ant Jokes

These jokes are based on the Aanaiyum Urumbum jokes popular in Kerala. In the original version, the ant and the elephant are friends, and the jokes are tall tales. Here are some examples:

- *Aana and Urumbu were playing hide-and-seek near a temple. Aana told the Urumbu that the temple was out of bounds for hiding. When they began playing, Aana had to seek and Urumbu could hide. Aana searched everywhere but could not find*

Urumbu. Aana became suspicious and decided to check the temple. It blocked the entrance and when the Urumbu sneaked back to capture the post, Aana caught him. How did Aana know that Urumbu was hiding in the temple? Urumbu's shoes were outside.

- *An aana was travelling on the road when it met with an accident. The ambulance took him to the hospital. An urumbu was seen following the ambulance on a motorcycle. What was the reason? To give blood for his injured friend, of course.*
- *One day, Aana and Urumbu went on a pilgrimage. When evening came, they decided to sleep under a tree. Aana could not sleep. What was the reason? Urumbu was snoring.*
- *Aana and Urumbu were travelling on a bike. They met with an accident. Aana died but Urumbu survived. How did that happen? Urumbu was wearing a helmet.*

In my version, the stories are tall tales but the two protagonists are (fr)enemies. It is not clear if Elephant is making up these stories and Ant is really innocent. That is left to your imagination.

- **Why did Elephant leave the cinema without watching the movie?**
  Ant was sitting in front of him and completely blocking his view.

- **Why could not Elephant climb up the stairs?**
  Ant was blocking the way.

- **Why could not Elephant get into the elevator?**
  - Ant and a rhino were already in the elevator. Ant pointed to a sign saying "Maximum: Two animals" and kicked Elephant out.

  - Every time Elephant tried to get in, Ant would sneak up behind it and tug at his tail.

- **How did Ant sabotage Elephant's car?**
  Whenever Elephant pressed the accelerator, Ant would lift the rear wheels a few inches off the ground.

- **What did Elephant complain to the TTE (Travelling Ticket Examiner)?"**
  Ant's luggage was placed all over his berth.

- **What did Elephant complain to the TTE of the train?"**
  Ant took his window seat.

- **Why did Elephant fall down the stairs?**
  Ant threw his weight around.

- **How did Elephant break his front leg?**
  Ant and Elephant were wearing the same colour of clothes so Ant pinched him.

- **How did Elephant land flat on the water surface?**
  Elephant was at the edge of the jumping platform, still preparing to jump, when Ant sneaked up behind him and started hopping wildly. Elephant lost his balance and fell awkwardly into the water.

- **How did Ant beat Elephant in a running race?**
  Ant at the beginning and the end of the race were lookalikes.

- **Why did Elephant get angry so early in the day?**
  Ant took his morning bath and used up all the water in the storage tank.

- **How did Elephant fall into the water?**
  Ant and Elephant went for a boat ride. After reaching the middle of the lake, Ant suddenly jumped out into the water and swam ashore. With nobody to counter-balance Elephant, the boat capsized.

- **How did Elephant fly through the air?**
  The same thing happened at the playground. Elephant was playing on the see-saw with Ant. Suddenly, Ant jumped off his seat.

- **How did Elephant fall on to the aisle?**
  When the bus went over a speed-breaker on the road, Ant side-bumped the dozing Elephant.

- **Why was Elephant limping on his feet?**
  Ant stepped on it by mistake.

- **What made Elephant fly off and smash into the wall?**
  Ant sneezed.

- **Before the Great Flood, Noah built his Ark and asked, "Is everyone on the list?"**
  His wife answered, "No. I asked the ant to write the list and it ignored the

elephant in the room."

- **Why did Elephant want to change his name?**
  There was an ant in it.

- **What did Elephant complain to the librarian?**
  Ant was reading loudly next to it.

- **Why was Elephant crying in the cafeteria of the school?**
  According to Elephant, Ant ate his candy and took his lunch money.

- **Why was Elephant upset after the school picnic?**
  The class was walking alongside a cliff. Elephant was at the end of the line.
  Elephant had stopped and was gingerly observing the steep fall from the top
  when Ant tapped him on the shoulder. Elephant almost jumped out of its skin.
  The subsequent conversation went like this:

  > **Elephant**: What do you want?
  > **Ant**: You know what will be good?
  > **Elephant**: What?
  > **Ant**: If you fell down this cliff!
  > **Elephant**: How will that be good?
  > **Ant**: You will make a good impression.

- **Why did Elephant refuse to go out?**
  - Ant was waiting outside to sell him insurance.
  - Ant was waiting outside to sign him up for organ donation.
  - Social distancing: Ant had coronavirus and was asking Elephant to come out
    and play with him.

Animal Jokes

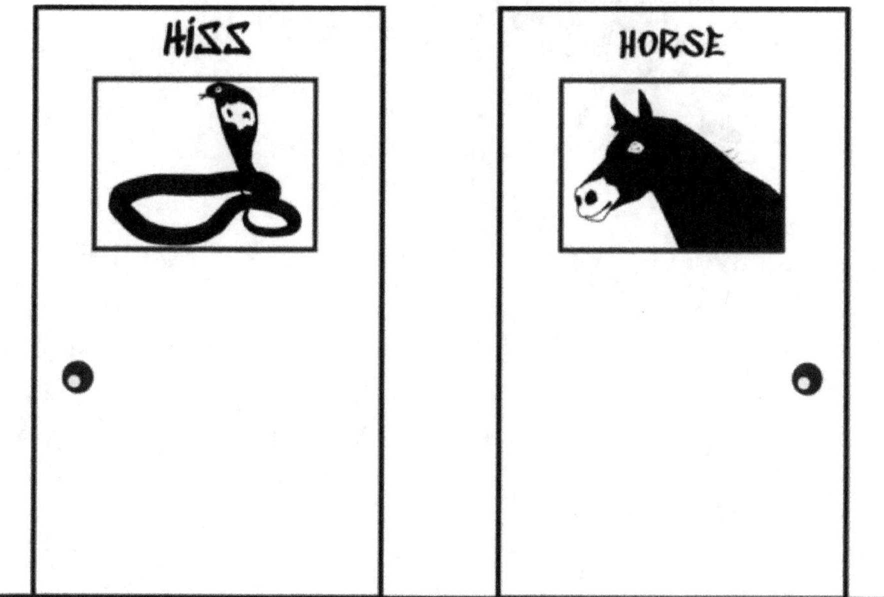

If you get to like the breakup jokes in this section, there is more in the section Romantic Jokes.

- **What happened to the anaconda after it had nothing to eat for several weeks?**
  It *sounded hollow*.

- **What did one ant say to another?**
  - "You and what army?"
  - "So, are you a Communist?"
  - "So, when are you flying?"
  - "I came here to grab a bite."
  - "Is it March already?"
  - "I have loads of work."
  - "The work here is not heavy."

- **What kind of music do alpacas like to listen?**
  Latin.

- **What kind of films do bats like to go to?**
  - Dark fantasy.
  - Silent pictures.

- **What kind of music do bed bugs like to listen to?**
  Ruggae.

- **What kind of music do bees like to listen?**

R&B.

- **Why did the policeman stop the stegosaurus?**
  To check his number plate.

- **What do cows like to read?**
  Bullion prices.

- **What do silverfish (book worms) like to read?**
  Pulp fiction.

- **What kind of music do frogs like to listen?**

Hip hop.

- **What kind of music do frogs hate to listen?**
  Instrumental.
- **What kind of live entertainment do dogs like to go to?**
  Puppetry.
- **What kind of films do duck like to go to?**
  Docudramas.
- **What kind of computer games do ducks hate to play?**
  Third-person shooter (TPS).
- **What kind of films do eagles like to read?**
  Legal dramas.
- **What kind of fiction do giraffes like to read?**
  Tall tales.
- **What kind of live entertainment do giraffes like to go to?**
  Stand-up comedies.
- **What do goats like to read?**
  Stock quotes.
- **What kind of computer games do lions like to play?**
  Real-time strategy.
- **What kind of films do mooses like to go to see?**
  Moosical.
- **What kind of eateries do owls hate to go to?**
  Owl-you-can-eat buffets.
- **What kind of live entertainment do owls like to see?**
  Snake charmer.
- **What kind of fiction do parrots like to read?**
  Parrodies.
- **What kind of music do rats like to listen?**
  Experimental.
- **What kind of films do roosters like to go to see?**
  Chick flicks.
- **What kind of films do sheep like to go to see?**
  Ramcoms.
- **What did one bat say to another?**
  "We should hang out sometimes."
- **What happened to the chipmunk that began to diet?**
  It *went nuts*.
- **How do you say boo to a duck?**
  In Portugeese.
- **Why did the giraffe refuse to leave the elevator?**
  It gets *lonely at the top*.
- **Why did the rhino use the elevator?**
  The stairs were swamped.
- **Why would the wildebeests of African savannah do well in the stock**

market?
They are *comfortable with large numbers*.

- **What was the ant doing in the farm equipment section?**
  It was a harvester ant.

- **What was the shark doing in the hardware section?**
  It was a sawtooth shark.

- **What was the shark doing in the women's clothing section?**
  It was a bonnethead shark.

- **What was the shark doing in the stationery section?**
  This was a loan shark.

- **What one firefly say to another?**
  "You gotta match, bud? I am out."

- **What did the fish say to the eel?**
  "Can you charge my phone?"

An electric eel is not really an eel.

- **What did the spider say to the insect?**
  "Thanks for dropping by."

- **What did one bull dog say to another?**
  "Why don't you smile?... Hey, what's with the sour expression?"

- **What did one chicken say to another?**
  "I think we are on the way to the market... Hey, what's with the fowl expression?"

- **What did one eel say to another?**
  "I am excited to meet you... Hey, what's with the shocked expression?"

- **What did one turkey say to another?**
  "We are nearing Thanksgiving... Hey, what's with the pained expression?"

- **What would happen if a draught animal came on the radio?**
  It would sound hoarse.

- **What would happen if a lion came on the radio?**
  It would be roaring fun.

- **What would happen if a pig came on the radio?**
  It would be boaring.

- **What would happen if a sheep came on the radio?**
  It would be really baaaaaad.

- **Why did the aardvark couple break up?**
  It had become very awkward between them.

- **Why did the alligator couple break up?**
  - He could not stand her grating remarks.
  - If he tried to say anything, she snapped at her.
  - When he cried, she dismissed it as crocodile tears.

- **How did the alpaca couple break up?**
  He said everything she said was all a pack of lies.

- **Why did the anaconda couple break up?**

- He could not swallow her insults anymore.
  - He did not have the guts to say 'no' to her.
  - He could not just lie there and pretend like nothing happened.
  - She was extremely unpredictable. She would chew him out for no reason.
- **Why did the ant couple break up?**
  - She insisted that every little thing he did was wrong.
  - He would not march to her beat.
  - He said there was not even a speck of truth in her allegations and she said that that was plenty.
  - He said that she may be an army ant but he was saluting nobody.
- **Why did the ant couple make up?**
  They did not want to let little things come between them.
- **Why did the anteater couple break up?**
  He could not stand her tongue-lashing.
- **Why did the antelope couple break up?**
  - They played hard-to-get for too long.
  - She accused him of running away from problems.
  - He suffered from an overwhelming desire to flee the relationship.
- **How did the antelope couple make up?**
  They endeered themselves to each other.
- **Why did the armadillo couple break up?**
  Even his tough exterior could not handle all the barbs she threw at him.
- **Why did the badger couple break up?**
  She said his relatives were originally all skunks.
- **Why did the bat couple break up?**
  - He went head-over-heels for her when they met but now he would not hang out anymore.
  - She accused him of placing all kinds of obstacles in her life.
  - She could not believe her eyes or ears when he said she was nuttier than a fruit bat.
  - Social distancing… after coronavirus… as if rabies was not bad enough!
  - They tried to rise above their differences but could not reach a compromise.
  - His repeated pleas for mercy fell on deaf ears.
  - They did not see it coming.
  - "I will never go on blind dates again."
- **Why did the bat couple make up?**
  - The breakup turned their world downside up.
  - They decided to ignore hangovers from the past.
  - Love is blind.
  - He listened.
- **Why did the bear couple break up?**
  - He could not make the bear-minimum to support a home.
  - He could not escape her bear hug every morning. [Thank you, Sheryl Crow.]
  - He would not call her 'honey' anymore. ("Don't 'honey' me, you big furry animal!")
  - He would play dead when asked to do housework.
  - He could not bear it anymore.

- o She was tired of his honeyed words.
- o He could not grin and bear it anymore.

- **How did the beaver couple break up?**
  She took the home and the kids, and left him with nothing.

- **Why did the bee couple break up?**
  - o She was constantly droning over nothing.
  - o She stung him when he was least expecting it.
  - o What was meant to be will be.
  - o He brought her flowers and she said, "Is this a joke?".

- **Why did the bee couple make up?**
  - o He promised to bee-have.
  - o They decided to let bee-gones be bee-gones.
  - o It is a private matter bee-tween them.

- **How did the bird couple break up?**
  He flew away at the first sign of trouble.

- **How did the bird couple make up?**
  Birds of a feather flock together.

- **Why did the boa constrictor couple break up?**
  - o It was overwhelming. He felt suffocated in that relationship.
  - o Her patience was stretched to the limit.
  - o Too early to say. They are still seized with the situation.
  - o She threatened to turn him inside out.
  - o They just could not get along with each other.
  - o She threatened to make him eat his tail and turn him into a ball.
  - o Everyday was a struggle for survival. He barely managed to hang in there.
  - o Her poisonous remarks left him frothing at the mouth.
  - o He could not stomach her insults anymore.
  - o His gut instinct told him to get out.

- **Why did the boa constrictor couple make up?**
  - o They felt torn apart by the separation.
  - o He promised to pay her close attention because she was one gorgeous boabe.
  - o He said his jokes about her size were made IN JEST.
  - o He promised to come back to her without any hang-ups from the past.
  - o She frankly admired his guts to say 'No' to her.
  - o They managed to squeeze out a compromise.
  - o He admitted he bit off more than he could chew.

- **Why did the buffalo couple break up?**
  - o He made quite a splash in the beginning. Now, he just wallows all the time.
  - o He described himself as tall, dark and handsome but she failed to note that he was no different from others.

- **Why did the camel couple break up?**
  It was the last straw.

- **Why did the cassowary couple break up?**
  'Cos, with every passing day, they grew more wary of each other.

- **Why did the cat couple break up?**
  - o They were on the fence about it for quite some time and finally took the

plunge in different directions.
  - They hated each other in all of their nine lives.
  - Don't worry about spilled milk.
  - She tried to make his life miserable but he always managed to land on his feet.

- **Why did the caterpillar couple break up?**
  She wanted spread her wings and transform into something new and different.

- **Why did the caterpillar couple make up?**
  He promised to turn a new leaf.

- **Why did the chameleon couple break up?**
  - He showed his true colours after the wedding.
  - She sees him in a different light now.
  - He had some butterflies in the stomach but he has had enough of her colourful remarks.
  - She could not believe how much he had changed.
  - He tried to blend in with the surroundings but she was too good for him and made him do housework.

- **Why did the cheetah couple break up?**
  There was no escaping her.

- **Why did the chicken couple break up?**
  - What he brought home was chickenfeed.
  - Around her, he felt like he was walking on eggshells all the time.

- **Why did the chicken couple make up?**
  - He did not want to raise her hackles.
  - He was her fowl-weather friend.

- **Why did the chimpanzee couple break up?**
  - He would scratch his head and grin from ear to ear but wouldn't understand a word she said.
  - She put him in a cardboard box and mailed it to NASA.

- **Why did the condor couple make up?**
  They were a married California condor couple, an endangered species.

- **Why did the cow couple break up?**
  - It was not cowardice. Her daily complaints were not moosic to his ears.
  - She wanted to be treated like a holy cow.
  - He would not be cowed down by her threats to make mincemeat out of him.
  - What he brought home was a 'big nothing burger'.
  - She routinely locked horns with him and it became a high-stakes game for survival.
  - He knew he was dead meat if he went home late.

- **Why did the crab couple break up?**
  - He barely managed to escape her death grip.
  - She welcomed him with open arms.

- **Why did the crab couple make up?**
  - He was a spineless fellow. He crawled back to her on all sixes.
  - She was like his right hand – big and strong.

- **Why did the crane couple break up?**
  He would not stick his neck out for her.

- **Why did the crocodile couple break up?**
  - They shed some crocodile tears and it was all over.
  - It was all a crock of lies.
  - They would open their mouths and refuse to shut up for hours.

- **Why did the crow couple break up?**
  - Even for a crow, she was very loud.
  - She was no hot chick but, when he compared her to a raven, she took it as a comment about her size.
  - Contrary to scientific studies, he was not very intelligent. And, quite a craven little birdie too.

- **Why did the donkey couple break up?**
  - Sometimes, he can be stubborn as an ass.
  - He was all ears for her then. Now, not so much anymore.
  - He would just stand there with a stupid smile on his face, like a jackass.

- **Why did the deer couple break up?**
  - They had too much weighing down on their heads.
  - He was tired of her hide-and-seek games.

- **Why did the dinosaur couple break up?**
  Once she becomes cold as ice, she just refuses to thaw.

- **Why did the dinosaur couple make up?**
  She said his brain must be as big as a matchbox.

- **Why did the duck couple break up?**
  - Bills, bills, bills, and more bills.
  - They both ducked the question.
  - He remained an ugly duckling forever.
  - She followed him everywhere he went.
  - When she gave her daily sermon, all he heard was, "Quack, quack, quack, quack, quack!"
  - If it walks like a duck and talks like a duck, then it hurts like a duck.
  - They took to it like duck to water.
  - In this economy, it is tough to stay afloat.

- **Why did the dog couple break up?**
  - "Her bark is worse than her bite. It should not happen to a dog."
  - Their relationship was best described as a dog-eat-dog situation.
  - She was breathing down his neck all the time.
  - She held him on a tight leash. He could not grin and wag his tail forever like that.
  - She expected him sit when she told him to sit and stand when she told him to stand.

- **Why did the dolphin couple break up?**
  There was no escaping her. Even when out of sight, he thought he could hear her.

- **Why did the dragon couple break up?**
  - They both breathed fire and burned down their homestead.
  - She gave him a serious case of heartburn.

- **Why did the duck couple make up?**

- He successfully floated the idea to her.
- Without her, he was a dead duck.

- **Why did the eagle couple break up?**
  - He felt he could never escape her constant gaze.
  - For a bald eagle, it was hair today and gone tomorrow.

- **Why did the electric eel couple break up?**
  - He thought he was making a positive approach but she took it negatively.
  - Shock and aaah!
  - Shocking... shocking failure to respect each other's personal space.
  - There seemed to be too much negative energy between them.
  - Probably for the shock value.

- **Why did the electric eel couple make up?**
  - He decided to test the waters again.
  - He said she was a slimy, lying, slithering and cold-blooded creature.

- **Why did the elephant couple break up?**
  - He was tall, dark and handsome but seriously overweight.
  - He failed to address the elephant in the room.
  - She trumpeted her achievements while he tried to stamp his authority.
  - "Elephants and women never forget."

From the poem by Dorothy Parker with the same title

- **Why did the elephant couple make up?**
  He can run but he can't hide.

- **Why did the eagle couple break up?**
  She endlessly picked on him and he felt an overwhelming desire to escape her clutches.

- **Why did the emu couple break up?**
  - He remained emmune to her advances.
  - He was emutionally insecure.
  - He would burst into tears at the mere sound of her footsteps.

- **How did the emu couple make up?**
  It was an *emutional roller coaster*.

- **What one firefly couple break up?**
  - The light had gone out of their relationship.
  - The fire had gone out of their relationship.

- **What one firefly couple make up?**
  He praised her in glowing terms.

- **Why did the fish couple break up?**
  - It's water under the bridge now.
  - She was such a clean freak that no matter how many baths he took it was not enough for her.
  - She carped on and on about how he was always wrapped up in a newspaper.

- **Why did the fish couple make up?**
  - She wanted to ACQUIRE HIM again.
  - He was a handsome catch.
  - The scales fell from her eyes.

- **Why did the flamingo couple break up?**
  He inflamed her passions initially. Now, not so much.
- **Why did the fly couple break up?**
  She would fly into a rage over nothing.
- **Why did the frog couple break up?**
  Every night, after he hopped over from the pub, she would hit the ceiling.
- **How did the frog couple break up?**
  He leapt with joy while she took a dive into depression.
- **Why did the frog couple make up?**
  She searched all over the swamp but she could not find a better specimen.
- **Why did the giraffe couple break up?**
  - When he came home late, she would hit the ceiling.
  - She set the bar too high for him.
- **Why did the goose couple break up?**
  What was good for the goose was not good for the gander.
- **Why did the gorilla couple break up?**
  She called him a 'stupid monkey'.

- **Why did the goat couple break up?**
  - He could not be goaded into doing her bidding.
  - He asked a vet if something could be done about her constant bleating.

- **Why did the hedgehog couple break up?**
    - He was tired of her barbs.
    - He did not have the spine to say no to her.
    - She knew he was not up to scratch.
    - She tried hard to make her point and it hurt.
- **Why did the hummingbird couple break up?**
    - He was tired of listening to her same old tune again and again.
    - They were out of tune with each other.
    - He struck a discordant note.
- **Why did the hummingbird couple make up?**
  He called her a bird-brain and she took it as a compliment.
- **Why did the hyena couple break up?**
    - They refused to laugh at each other's jokes.
    - He had nothing to counter her biting remarks.
    - What he brought home was just scraps.
- **What do hyenas like to read?**
  The funny papers.
- **Why did the crested ibis couple break up?**
  She wanted to be treated like a *sacred ibis*.

- **Why did the hadeda ibis couple break up?**
  They yelled at each other all the time.

- **Why did the hornet couple break up?**
  He had nothing to counter her stinging accusations.
- **Why did the jellyfish couple break up?**
  He desperately wanted to escape her tentacles.
- **Why did the Komodo dragon couple break up?**
  There was no fire in the relationship.
- **Why did the koel couple break up?**
  He was a total 'cuckoo for brains'.
- **Why did the lice couple break up?**
  She said he was gross and he called her a parasite.
- **Why did the lice couple make up?**
    - They took it as a compliment.
    - It is a jungle out there. Two heads are better than one.
- **Why did the lion couple break up?**
    - He refused to shave.
    - If she caught him roaming outside, she made him stand on a stool.
- **Why did the lion couple make up?**
  Outside, he roared like a lion. Inside the house, when she cracked the whip, he put his tail between his legs like a dog and moved around like a mouse.
- **How did the llama couple break up?**

They walked away, looked back, and spat each other's direction.

- **Why did the Barbary lion couple break up?**
  They were on their way out anyway.

- **Why did the lizard couple break up?**
  She drove him up the wall.

- **Why did the woolly mammoth couple break up?**
  He had grown long in the tooth.

- **Why did the mice couple break up?**
  - He brought cheese straight from the factory but she was still not satisfied with his cooking.
  - He couldn't see the writing on the wall.
  - She asked him if he was a mouse or a man when he said he was tired of eating cheese every day.

- **If a mice wanted to read detective fiction, what book would it read?**
  Who moved my cheese?

- **Why did the mole couple break up?**
  - She made a mountain out of a molehill.
  - He finally dug his way out of her maze of traps.
  - She does not dig him any more.

- **Why did the moose couple break up?**
  When they first met, he said he was an artist and she could be her muse. Now, he just wants her out of the picture.

- **Why did the musk ox couple break up?**
  Her talks always gave him a headache.

- **Why did the narwhal couple break up?**
  She struck him as unfriendly.

- **Why did the nightingale couple break up?**
  He was singing the same old song like a broken record.

- **Why did the octopus couple break up?**
  - She had too much on her hands.
  - He would not lend her a hand while doing housework.
  - He caught her on the wrong foot.
  - He lost all his earnings buying her shoes.
  - He was too many problems in his hands and it all came to a head.
  - She challenged him to a battle of wits and he commended her for coming unarmed.

- **What did the mother octopus say to the baby octopuses?**
  "Kids, will you stop it? I have only eight arms."

- **Why did the ostrich couple break up?**
  - He decided to make a run for it.
  - Protecting the world's biggest eggs is no easy task.
  - Whenever she complained, he would bury his head in the ground.

- **Why did the ostrich couple make up?**

- o She caught up with him.
  - o He can run but he cannot hide.
- **Why did the otter couple break up?**
  Every time she wanted to talk, he would roll over and go to sleep.
- **Why did the owl couple break up?**
  - o She nagged him day and night.
  - o The relationship screeched to a halt.
- **Why did the owl couple make up?**
  Owl is fair in love and war.
- **Why did the parrot couple break up?**
  She would repeat the same old complaints again and again, imitating his own voice.
- **What kind of music do parrots like to listen?**
  Pirated.
- **Why did the pelican couple break up?**
  He was tired of her big mouth.
- **Why did the pig couple break up?**
  - o He was quite a boar.
  - o She would wade in to the living room and hog the remote during the last over.
  - o Living with her was like being hog-tied all the time.
- **Why did the polar bear couple break up?**
  - o The very thought of him made her shudder.
  - o The very thought of her made him break into a sweat.
- **Why did the porcupine couple break up?**
  - o She would needle him over nothing.
  - o He remained a thorn on her side.
  - o She struck him as a tad unfriendly.
  - o She had a painful way of making her point across.
- **How did the porcupine couple break up?**
  - o He bought a water bed.
  - o He would make up all kinds of false stories and she would put all kinds of holes in them.
- **Why did the possum couple break up?**
  She threatened to betray him to some starving hillbilly.
- **Why did the python couple break up?**
  Under pressure, he just choked.
- **How did the python couple break up?**
  - o They are still mentally digesting what happened.
  - o They were crushed.
  - o After they met, she had him wrapped around her finger in no time.
- **Why did the python couple make up?**
  - o He bit off more than he could chew.
  - o She was not the one to give up so quickly.
  - o She made a mind-numbing jaw-dropping offer to take him back.

- **How did the quail couple break up?**
  - What he brought home was chickenfeed.
  - She accused him of being a chicken.
- **Why did the rabbit couple break up?**
  She was swift with the repartee and he was quick to take offence.
- **How did the raccoon couple break up?**
  She said she had seen his photo on a 'Wanted for burglary' poster and he said he hoped she will make a good hat.
- **Why did the rat couple break up?**
  - He promised her a nice place in the city but they were still living on a dump in the outskirts.
  - He felt trapped in that marriage.
  - She was not attracted by his cheesy humour anymore.
  - What he brought home could not even feed a mouse.
- **Why did the rhinoceros couple break up?**
  She said that, even though he had two of them, his horns did not match and they were on the wrong side of his head.
- **Why did the rhinoceros couple make up?**
  She promised not to make pointed remarks and he believed she had honourable intentions.
- **Why did the salmon couple break up?**
  She was tired of his canned replies.
- **Why did the scorpion couple break up?**
  Her comments stings like a scorpion.
- **Why did the seal couple break up?**
  He refused to dance to her tune.
- **Why did the secretary bird couple break up?**
  He noted that she was acting more and more like a dictator.
- **Why did the shark couple break up?**
  - The shark is the most cunning hunter in water. All the more difficult for a male shark when his mate can sense him from a mile away.
  - There are many deadly predators in the sea. For him, it was the open ocean or her. He chose the ocean.
  - He considered her as a trophy wife.
  - She says he hoped she would become a trophy.
  - He was a different kettle of fish.
  - He escaped from her by the skin of his teeth.
  - Her bark was worse than her bite.
- **How did the sheep couple break up?**
  - He was shorn of any responsibility.
  - She followed him everywhere.
- **How did the silverfish couple break up?**
  - He was always buried in his books.
  - He took a bite out of her book.
- **How did the shellfish couple break up?**

He accused her of being selfish.

- **Why did the sloth couple break up?**
  He was sloth to compliment her.

- **Why did the snail couple break up?**
  o Her pace was too much for him.
  o He made a quick getaway as best as he could.
  o She said he was cruising for a bruising.

- **Why did the snail couple make up?**
  o They felt that a change of pace was better than rushing into uncharted territory.
  o He promised to make serious progress.

- **Why did the snake couple break up?**
  o Peel that outer layer and you find a total reptile inside!
  o He will make your skin crawl.
  o He was like something that crawled out from under a rock.
  o He could not stand her accusations lying down.
  o The relationship had become too toxic.
  o He was a total creep.
  o He would not dance to her tune.
  o She made his blood boil.
  o Oh, the things she said would make a snake stand on its tail!

- **Why did the snake couple make up?**
  o He said that, if there was one lying slithering cold-blooded reptile he could not forget, it was her.
  o They decided to let past infractions slide.
  o He charmed his way back into her heart.

- **Why did the spider couple break up?**
  He didn't want to get caught in her web of deceit and treachery.

- **Why did the squirrel couple break up?**
  o She was nuts about him once but now thinks she was just nuts.
  o What he brought home was peanuts.
  o This nut was not complimentary.

- **Why did the starfish couple break up?**
  o They literally broke up.
  o It was written in the stars.

- **Why did the stick insect couple break up?**
  o She wanted to stick it to that creep.
  o She threw all kinds of allegations at him but nothing would stick.

- **Why did the stick insect couple make up?**
  He loved her so much that he would not stick up for himself.

- **Why did the stingray couple break up?**
  He had no answer to her stinging remarks.

- **Stork couple breakup**

  Stork 1: That couple had broken up.
  Stork 2: What happened?
  Stork 1: She tried to pull his leg.

Stork 2: Just because of a joke?
Stork 1: No, she pulled the leg he was standing on.

- **Why did the stork couple break up?**
  - It was time for a stork to take a stand and put his foot down.
  - His painting did not match the décor of her home.

- **Why did the swan couple break up?**
  They became swan enemies.

- **Why did the swan couple break up?**
  He is her swan song in this life.

- **Why did the tadpole couple break up?**
  She did not like his juvenile attitude.

- **Why did the tadpole couple make up?**
  He promised her that he will try to become a mature individual.

- **Why did the tick couple break up?**
  Every time he opened his mouth to say something, she ticked him off.

- **Why did the tortoise couple break up?**
  His silent treatment was killing her. Whenever she talked, he would close his eyes and withdraw into his shell.

- **Why did the tortoise couple make up?**
  - Without her, he became a broken shell of a tortoise.
  - She dropped the bombshell on his back but he did not crack.

- **Why did the toad couple break up?**
  He croaked under the pressure.

- **How did the toucan couple break up?**
  He put his beak where it did not belong.

- **Why did the turkey couple break up?**
  He thought she was fattening him up for a Christmas surprise.

- **Why did the turkey couple break up?**
  It was nearing Thanksgiving and he said she looked fat.

- **Why did the turtle couple break up?**
  Whenever she talked, he would turn turtle and go to sleep.

- **How did the whale couple break up?**
  They had a whale of a time together but now it is all over.

- **Why did the white ant couple break up?**
  He could not afford to have a roof over their heads.

- **How did the walrus couple break up?**
  Tsk! Tsk! Tsk! Tsk!

- **How did the walrus couple break up?**
  He was getting long in the tooth.

- **How did the wolf couple break up?**
  He let out a howl and danced with joy.

- **How did the yak couple break up?**

He would yack away all the time and not let her get in a word.

- **How did the zebra couple break up?**
  He crossed her the wrong way.

- **What did the ant say to the anteater?**
  o "Why don't you pick someone your own size?"
  o "Well, if you are that then go and eat your aunt!"

- **What happens if you give neodymium to birds?**
  You get chick magnets.

- **Why did the moth see the doctor?**
  He was feeling suicidal, usually in the presence of a fire.

- **Depression Hotline**

    Caller: The holidays are coming and I am feeling depressed.
    Counsellor: Unless you are a turkey, there is no need to feel depressed.
    Caller: [Sound of a turkey crying followed by a click]

- **Holy Cows**
  Cows are not unusual sight on Indian roads but it seems to fascinate Western tourists. So, here is a real story about some Indian cows. It was reported in *The Hindu*. Rajaji Salai is a very busy place, given that it is near the port, the Fort, the High Court, Burma Bazaar, bank offices and the business district. Among the fixtures on this road were several cows. One day, one of them was knocked down by a bus. Usually, when a cow is on the road, living or dead, the traffic arches around the animal and proceeds at a slower pace. In this instance, however, something strange happened. The news of the dead cow seems to have spread like wildfire. Cows from all around the area trudged to the site of the accident. They stood around the dead cow in silent protest and mourning. Traffic on the arterial road was held up for several hours.

- **CatNav**
  One day, back when I was kid, I found a newborn kitten at a building that was under construction. I took it home and it became our pet. It was a good cat but had one bad habit. On days when fish was cooked, the cat acted like it was possessed by some evil spirit. This was not a problem until a day when a guest arrived. Fish was on the menu and the cat caused serious embarrassment. It would not let the man eat in peace. It would scratch at the door, make unworldly noises and demanded to be let it in. After the guest left, a decision was made to get rid of the cat. I was the one tasked with it. A relative would accompany me to the other side of the railway track, several kilometres from the home, and I was supposed to abandon it. I literally let the cat out of the bag there. As we scooted back from the scene on our cycle, I saw the cat stand there wondering what was happening. I was brokenhearted. I need not have worried. Next day, I woke up to the familiar sounds of the cat. How did it return? It must have had made a mental map of smells and traced its way back, somehow avoiding hundreds of dogs, cats and vehicles.

Fancy Creature Jokes

Everyone likes fairy tales. The *Panchatantra* is the source of many fairy tales in which animals speak like humans. While many foreign cultures have borrowed from it, they have their own unique fancy creatures and tales. Ireland has the banshee. Scotland has the Loch Ness monster. Vampires are popular all over the Western world. Here are a few jokes about many such creatures.

- **What does** ABOMINABLE SNOWMAN**'s school yearbook say about him?**
  "Most likely to leave quite a trail."

- **The** ABOMINABLE SNOWMAN **walks into a bar**
  The Abominable Snowman walks into a bar and orders a drink. The bartender says, "That'll be twenty bucks." The Snowman is shocked and says, "This is an abomination."

- **Why did** wailing banshee **retire?**
  It was a crying shame.

- A screaming banshee **walks into a bar**
  A banshee walks into a bar and says, "I am dying for a drink." The barman pours it some brandy. When the banshee finishes the drink, the barman asks, "How is it now?" The banshee replies, "It's nothing to cry about."

- **What did the** wailing banshee **say?**
  Just mourning.

- **What does** BATMAN**'s school yearbook say about him?**
  "Most likely to hang out it with shady characters."

- Bogeyman
  > **Mrs. Bogeyman**: Sometimes, you scare me.
  > **Mr. Bogeyman**: No, honey, you are imaginary things!

- **What does** COUNT DRACULA**'s school yearbook say about him?**
  "Most likely to live life to the fullest."

- **What is** COUNT DRACULA**'s favourite self-help book?**
  How to stop worrying and start living.

- **What was the last thing the psychiatrist said to** COUNT DRACULA**?**
  "Now, I would like you to do some personal reflection."

- Cyclops
  > **Mother cyclops**: Make sure your brother does not get his clothes dirty.
  > **Daughter cyclops**: Don't worry, Mom. I have my eye on him.

- A cyclops **walks into a bar**
  A cyclops walks into a bar and the bartender says, "What can I get ye?"

- **What does** EGYPTIAN MUMMY**'s school yearbook say about him?**
  "Most likely to leave a lasting legacy."

- **An** EGYPTIAN MUMMY **walks into a bar**
  - An Egyptian mummy walks into a bar and orders a drink. While he is drinking, the barman asks, "So, what's your story?" The mummy looks up from his drink and says, "A riches-to-rags one, I suppose."
  - An Egyptian mummy walks into a bar and the barman says, "Long time, no see." The mummy says, "Sorry, I was all tied up."

- **Why did the** EGYPTIAN MUMMY **couple break up?**

It was bound to happen.

- *Fairies*

  Fairy 1: How well can you fly?
  Fairy 2: Fairly well.

- **What kind of music does the Grim Reaper like to listen?**
  Soul.

- **What does hydra's school yearbook say about him?**
  "Most likely to have the best head in the business."

- **What made the hydra couple break up?**
  It was not so much that she had nine heads to dish out her daily list of complaints but that he had eighteen ears to listen. He tried to let her complaints in through one ear and out through the other without much thought, but when he let it out from one head, it inevitably entered another head. He tried severing a head but two new heads always grow in its place, compounding his problem.

- **A hydra walks into a bar**
  A hydra walks into a bar and orders nine glasses of beer. The conversation with the bartender goes like this:

  Do you ever feel that you should cut it?
  The drinks?
  No.
  The heads?
  No. Never mind."

- **Imps**

  Mr. Imp: Did you see the remote?
  Mrs. Imp: It didn't tell me when it went out.
  Mr. Imp: Oh, you are impossible!

- **What does Loch Ness monster's school yearbook say about him?**
  "Most likely to rise above the rest."

- **A Loch Ness monster walks into a bar**
  A Loch Ness monster walks into a bar and orders a whisky. The bartender asks, "Any particular label?" Nessie replies, "Anything to drown my sorrows and disappear."

- **What did the nymph say to the mermaid?**
  "Will you blink once in a while? You have that dead fish look in your eyes."

- **SASQUATCH**

  Sasquatch 1: Did you talk to that cute one you were following?
  Sasquatch 1: No. She gave me the brush.

- **What does the siren's school yearbook say about her?**
  "Most likely to steal our hearts."

- **What does Spiderman's school yearbook say about him?**
  "Most likely to scale great heights."

- **What does SUPERMAN's school yearbook say about him?**
  "Most likely to come out with flying colours."

- **What does the _THUNDERBIRD_'s yearbook say about him?**
  "Most likely to kick up a storm."

- **What does the TROLL's school yearbook say about him?**
  "Most likely to carry a lot of weight in his circle."

- **What did one TROLL say to another after they were exposed to sunlight?**
  "What's with the stony expression?"

- **What does TROLL's school yearbook say about him?**
  "Most likely to rock our world."

- **A TROLL walks into a bar**
  A troll walks into a bar late at night but stays in the shadow behind the door. "Kill the lights and give me a drink," the troll hollers. The bartender turns off the switches and pours a drink. He slides the drink to the end of the bar and says, "Here is some light beer."

- **What happened to the TROLL during the storm?**
  There was a lightning storm and he was petrified for a whole minute.

- **What does vampire's school yearbook say about him?**
  "Most likely to suck at the one thing he does best."

- **What does a vampire call a blood bank?**
  Food bank.

- **Why do vampires always bite in the neck?**
  It is wrong to bite the hand that feeds you.

- **A vampire walks into a bar**
  A vampire walks into a bar and the bartender asks, "Need a drink?" The vampire replies, "No, I just dropped in for a bite."

- **A WEREWOLF walks into a bar**
  A werewolf walks into a bar and the bartender asks sarcastically, "You also dropped in for a bite?" The werewolf shakes his head, "No, I am here for the leftovers."

- **Another WEREWOLF walks into a bar**
  Another werewolf walks into a bar and the bartender asks, "And, what are you here for?" The werewolf points to the werewolf from the previous joke and says, "I have a bone to pick with him."

- **What does WEREWOLF's school yearbook say about him?**
  "Most likely to cause serious changes in society."

- **A Yeti walks into a bar**
  A Yeti walks into a bar and orders a drink. Everyone becomes nervous. To ease the mood, the Yeti asks the bartender, "Seen anything strange tonight?" The bartender replies, "Nothing **YET**, I suppose."

Geography Jokes

The country-specific jokes in this section are questions framed like a *National Geographic* quiz. But, there are no facts in question, just logic. That is, logic in the misleading style of 'Archie' of *Duffy's Tavern*. It is somewhat like a crossword puzzle clue. (To learn more about *Duffy's Tavern*, read the article *Vintage Radio Shows* on my website.) The questions are most fun if one

*person poses these questions to a group before reading the answer.*

- **Why did the flat-earther couple break up?**
  He drove her to the edge all the time but this time she felt that he had gone too far.

- **How does good news become bad news for a volcano?**
  Because it may erupt with joy.

- **Why did the geologist couple break up?**
  - It was a rocky relationship.
  - He felt like he was caught between a rock and a hard place.
  - Their relationship had hit rock bottom.

- **Why did the geologist couple make up?**
  It was uncharted territory for them.

- **What kind of music do geologists like to listen?**
  Just plain rock.

- **What kind of music do drunk geologists like to listen?**
  Rock-n-roll.

- **What kind of music do divorced geologists like to listen?**
  Alternative rock.

- **How did seismologist couple break up?**
  They were devastated.

- **Why did seismologist couple break up?**
  - It was a disaster to begin with.
  - He trembled with fear at the mere sound of her footsteps.
  - When anything went wrong, it was always his fault.

- **Not on my plate**

  Continental Plate 1: Did you cause that earthquake?
  Continental Plate 2: No, it's your fault.

- **What can you do with two globes?**
  Make the best of both worlds.

- **Name the Asian country that is named after a type of blanket or shawl.**
  Afghanistan.

- **Name the landlocked Asian country with a long history of people being mean to it.**
  Armenia.

- **Name the European country that is named after the ostrich bird.**
  Austria.

- **Name the English-speaking country that is so lazy and laid back that they copied from a country that was named after the ostrich.**
  Australia.

- **Name the Caribbean nation that is even more laid back than Australia that they cannot even say "Bah! Humbug!"**
  Bahamas.

- Name the Middle Eastern nation that is so parched that where everyone scoffs at the very idea of rain.
  Bahrain.
- Name the Caribbean country which was founded by a hair stylist who banned Afros and made two haircuts mandatory per year.
  Barbados.
- Which country hosts the largest number of Internet bots?
  Botswana.
- Name the European country that causes heartburn all over Europe.
  Belgium.
- If you said this South American country was founded by a girl named Olivia nobody would believe ya.
  Bolivia.
- Name the oil-rich South-East Asian country where the local brew will make you neigh like a horse?
  Brunei.
- Which East European country has been afflicted with a special strain of malaria whose chief symptom is bloating?
  Bulgaria.
- Name the African country that can so bore you to death that pathologically overexcited people go there to calm down.
  Burundi.
- Which African country is the largest manufacturer of the burkini, the Middle-Eastern head-to-toe version of the bikini?
  Burkina Faso.
- Which South-East Asian country where the most photogenic people live?
  Cambodia.
- Name the African country that was once a penal colony for people convicted of causing accidents with selfie sticks.
  Cameroon.
- Which country is the largest manufacturer of canned food?
  Canada.
- Which equatorial African country was named after an automobile?
  CAR (Central African Republic).
- Which South American country was named after a hot spice?
  Chile.
- Which Asian country is named after high-quality porcelain dishes?
  China.
- To which African country can you never go?
  Congo.
- To which African republic can you never go?
  Republic of Congo.
- Name the African country on the Atlantic ocean that is a favourite destination for perpetual worriers?
  Ivory Coast.

- In which Caribbean country do people live in houses made of ice cubes?
  Cuba.

- In which European country do people never check their spelling?
  Czechia (formerly Czech Republic, which sadly broke off from Czechoslovakia).

- In which European country where the national IQ has never crossed 10?
  Denmark.

- Which Caribbean country where everyone lives in dome-shaped houses?
  Dominica.

- Which Caribbean republic where everyone lives in dome-shaped houses?
  Dominican Republic.

- Which South American country was founded by Salvador Dali's evil twin?
  Ecuador.

- In which West African country, do they make you to drink gin up to this?
  Equatorial Guinea.

- In which East African which country, do they get easily irritated?
  Eritrea.

- In which East European country, do they stone you to death for ordinary crimes?
  Estonia.

- Which African country was the first one in Africa to form a S.W.A.T. unit?
  Eswatini (fomerly Swaziland).

- Which country in Europe is famed for its fish consumption?
  Finland.

- In which African country do people yack away like no tomorrow?
  Gabon.

- In which African country is gambling a way of life?
  Gambia.

- Which former Soviet republic's entire economy was originally based on postal packages originally destined for a province in the U.S.A.?
  Georgia.

- Which European country has the best defence against many germs?
  Germany.

- What can you do if your geographical knowledge is a bit rusty?
  You apply some Greece.

- Which Caribbean state was left grumbling when they realized that the name 'Canada' was already taken?
  Grenada.

- Which Caribbean country has the largest number of haters outside it?
  Haiti.

- In which European country was named to divert food aid after the devastation caused by World War I?
  Hungary.

- Which North Atlantic country is known as the 'Land of the Frozen Water'?
  Iceland.

- **Which Asian country was originally populated by Native Americans?**
  India.

- **Which South American country was so named because the confusion caused by countries named Guinea was not enough?**
  Guyana.

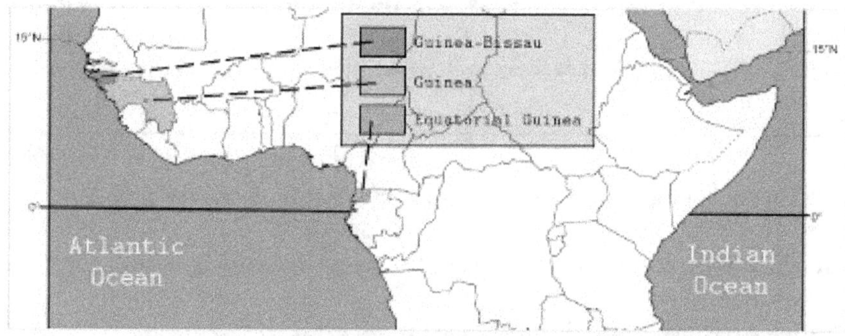

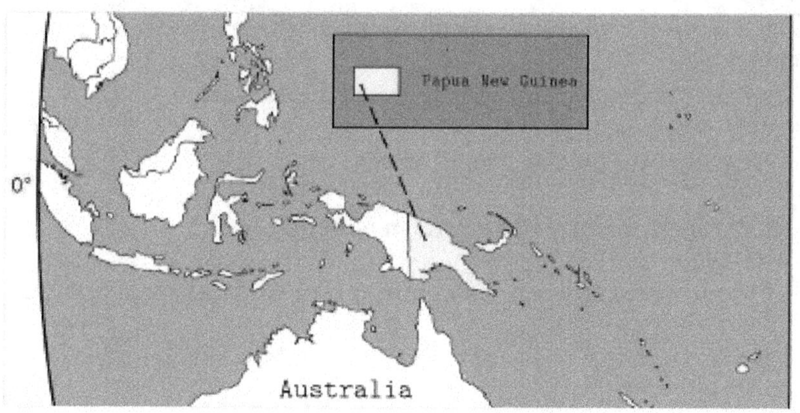

Some countries in Western Africa region are named after the around Gulf of Guinea. Papua New Guinea in the Oceanic region is so named because Spanish explorers thought the natives resembled the African people of Guinea.

- **Which Asian country stretches between between India and Malaysia?**
  Indonesia.

- **Name the Middle-Eastern country that Americans think has to be pronounced as an eye that ran away.**
  Iran.

It is all right to say EE-RAAHN. People in the Middle East seem to pronounce it as EH-RAAHN.

- **Name the Middle-Eastern country that Americans think has to be pronounced as a rack to showcase eyes.**
  Iraq.

- **Which European country has earned the ire of Iranians and Iraqis for causing Americans mispronounce their country's name?**
  Ireland.

- **Which country in the Middle East was the first to have a railway system?**
  Israel.

- **Which European country is named after the South-Indian dish '*idli*'?**
  Italy.

- **Which South-East Asian country is always lost in chaos?**
  Laos.

- **In which East European country are the people habitually late?**
  Latvia.

- **Which African country is on the east of Siberia?**
  Liberia.

- **Which European tax haven is the birthplace of the Frankenstein monster?**
  Liechtenstein.

- **Which East European country has highest literacy rate?**
  Lithuania.

- **Which country was moulded out of an egg?**
  Moldova.

- **Which European country is straight out of hell?**
  Netherlands.

- **Which is the newest country built entirely over land reclaimed from sea?**
  New Zealand.

- **Which Arab country has earned the ire of feminists for being named after the greatness of Man?**
  Oman.

- **Which South Asian country is packed with guys named Stanley?**
  Pakistan.

- **Name the European country where almost every citizen is mistaken for being very refined, cultured and polished?**
  Poland.

- **Which European country is named after female sailors?**
  Portugal.

- **In which European country do you find the most number of rowing fanatics?**
  Romania.

- **In which Eurasian country do people tend to rush ya?**
  Russia.

- **In which South East Asian country are ties important?**

Thailand.

- **In which Oceanian country, do people eat with tongs?**
  Tonga.

- **In which East African country do people greet each other with "You again, duh"?**
  Uganda.

- **Which former Soviet republic gets blamed when floods inundate the United Kingdom?**
  Ukraine.

- **Which English-speaking European country has the dullest and most generic name?**
  United Kingdom.

- **Which country in the western hemisphere pretends like it is a continent?**
  United States of America.

- **If a national capital could change into a girl and still retain its Christian name, what would it be?**
  Hint: The capital of Bulgaria.

- **How to remember stalagmite**

    Stalactite: What are you wondering?
    Stalagmite: Whether I **might** reach the ceiling.

- **How to remember stalactite**

    Stalagmite: What are you looking for?
    Stalactite: For a **site** to stand on.

- **How does magma fight?**
  "You and me. Let's take this outside."

- **How does lava fight?**
  "Cool it, man. Forget what happened down there."

- **Who are the 2% of scientists who advocate Climate Change rather than oppose it?**
  Psychiatrists who prescribe to their patients that a change in climate would be a good thing.

- **From the *Train Atlas***
  In 2003, I bought the *Atlas* from a railway station and found these facts under the title *Indian Railways: Some Fascinating Facts* and the facts were indeed fascinating.
  - Indian railways has the widest rail tracks in the world. The British chose the 5-feet 6-inch gauge as the standard because many parts of the country was prone to cyclones and flooding. This gauge was considered more safe than the standard gauge used all over the world. Some other countries such as Pakistan and Bangladesh use the Indian gauge as the national standard.
  - The shortest station name for a station is Ib, near Jharsuguda, on the Howrah-Nagpur main line.
  - The longest station name is Srivenkatanarasimharajuvariapeta on the Arakkonam-Renigunta section of the Southern Railway, which is the first station after Renigunta onward to Bombay.
  - The Himsagar Express between Jammu Tawi (Jammu & Kashmir) and

Kanyakumari (Tamil Nadu) has the longest run both in terms of total time taken and distance covered. It covers its route of 2,344 miles in 74 hours and 55 minutes.

- The Prayagraj Express, with 26 coaches, is the longest train in the country.
- The Haldia-Asansol Express, which has just three coaches, is the shortest train and is, oddly, often hauled by the powerful WAP-4 locomotive.
- Ghoom near Darjeeling in West Bengal is the highest station at 2,258 meters, or 7,407 feet.
- People afraid of tunnels should not take the Karbude tunnel on the Konkan Railway along the west coast, which is the longest tunnel at 4.06 miles.
- The Godavari bridge near Rajahmundry in Andhra Pradesh, which stretches 3.125 miles, is the longest.

Jokes You Love To Hate

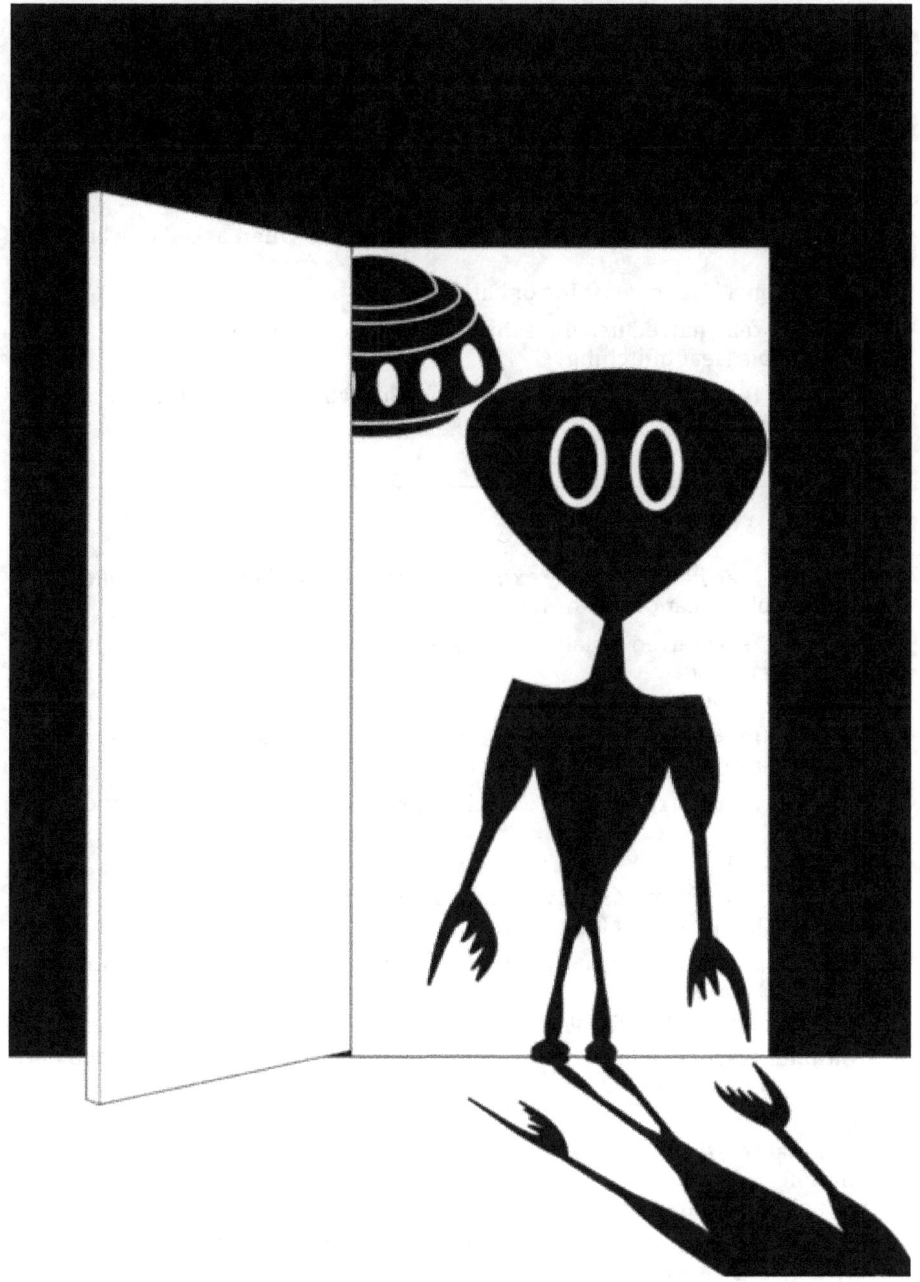

Phobia is Latin for fear. It's opposite, *mania*, stands for attraction.

- **Irrational fear/hatred usually exhibited by a pirate when asked to walk the plank**
  Ablutophobia [fear of washing or bathing]

- **Irrational fear/hatred usually exhibited by a recovering alcoholic**
  Acarophobia [fear of itching]

- **Irrational fear/hatred exhibited by some kids when their father offers them lemon drink**
  Acerophobia [fear of sourness]

- **Irrational fear/hatred usually exhibited by fireflies when they run out of gas**
  Achluophobia [fear of darkness]

- **Irrational fear/hatred usually exhibited by kids when they try to eat hard candy discreetly**
  Acousticophobia [fear of noise]

- **Irrational fear/hatred usually exhibited by climbers during an avalanche**
  Acrophobia or altophobia [fear of heights]

- **Irrational fear/hatred usually exhibited by hijackers after the ATF shoots all the tyres**
  Aerophobia [fear of flying]

- **Irrational fear/hatred usually lacking in drivers who drink**
  Aeroacrophobia [fear of high and open places]

- **Irrational fear/hatred usually exhibited by a flycatcher bird after it snags a stink bug by mistake**
  Aeronausiphobia [fear of vomiting in high places]

- **Irrational fear/hatred usually exhibited by people when they watch the evening debates on TV**
  Agateophobia [fear of going mad]

- **Irrational fear/hatred usually exhibited by people when they fall into a manhole**
  Agoraphobia [fear of open places]

- **Irrational fear/hatred usually exhibited by smartphone addicts**
  Agyrophobia [fear of crossing streets]

- **Irrational fear/hatred usually exhibited by balloons**
  Aichmophobia [fear of sharp or pointy things]

- **Irrational fear/hatred usually exhibited by goldfish when a four-legged creature looks intently at the tank**
  Ailurophobia [fear of cats]

- **Irrational fear/hatred usually exhibited by bungee jumpers**
  Agliophobia or algophobia [fear of pain]

- **Irrational fear/hatred usually exhibited by women married to men suffering from entomophobia**
  Alektorophobia [fear of chicken]

- **Irrational fear/hatred usually exhibited by people when they find a line of ants leading to an ice-cream cone they forgot to eat last night**
  Entomophobia [fear of insects]

- **Irrational fear/hatred usually taken advantage of by vampire hunters**
  Alliumphobia [fear of garlic]

- **Irrational fear/hatred usually exhibited by terrorists when Internet users viciously condemn them by changing the colour of some icons**
  Allodoxaphobia [fear of opinions]

- **Irrational fear/hatred usually exhibited by clean-freaks in any place except their room**
  Amathophobia [fear of dust]

- **Irrational fear/hatred usually exhibited by people when they forget their license at home**
  Amaxophobia [fear of driving in a vehicle]

- **Irrational fear/hatred usually exhibited by soldiers when they translate a sign and find that it says 'DANGER LANDMINES'**
  Ambulophobia [fear of walking]

- **Irrational fear/hatred usually exhibited by people after they change their password**
  Amnesiphobia [fear of amnesia]

- **Irrational fear/hatred usually exhibited by mobile phone store personnel when they have to take a new phone from a sealed package for demonstration to just one customer**
  Amychophobia [fear of scratches] and haphephobia [fear of touch]

- **Irrational fear/hatred usually exhibited by politicians who have been voted out and the new government is working wonders to the economy**
  Anablephobia [fear of looking up]

- **Irrational fear/hatred usually exhibited by builders of card pyramids**
  Ancraophobia or anemophobia [fear of wind]

- **Irrational fear/hatred usually exhibited by feminists**
  Androphobia [fear of men]

- **Irrational fear/hatred usually exhibited by most married men**
  Gynophobia [fear of women]

- **Irrational fear/hatred usually exhibited by bubbles**
  Aphenphosmphobia [fear of touch]

- **Irrational fear/hatred usually exhibited by an antelope when it runs from a cheetah**
  Aphenphosmphobia [fear of intimacy]

- Irrational fear/hatred exhibited by tourists when they fall into piranha-infested rivers
  Aquaphobia [fear of water]

- Irrational fear/hatred usually exhibited by levitating psychics
  Astraphobia [fear of thunder and lightning]

- Irrational fear/hatred usually exhibited by suicide bombers when the explosion causes extensive damage but fails to kill them
  Atelophobia [fear of flaws/imperfection]

- Irrational fear/hatred usually exhibited by kids when they leave their beach castles
  Atephobia [fear of ruins or ruination]

- Irrational fear/hatred usually exhibited by kids when parents forget to buy icecream during family outings
  Athazagoraphobia [fear of being forgotten or ignored]

- Irrational fear/hatred usually exhibited by small kids when they eat popping candy
  Atomosophobia [fear of atomic explosions]

- Irrational fear/hatred usually exhibited by electronic products manufactured for planned obsolescence
  Atychiphobia [fear of failure]

- Irrational fear/hatred usually exhibited by flautists when they walk into a curtain and hit a closed door
  Aulophobia [fear of flutes]

- Irrational fear/hatred usually exhibited by tax evaders during a raid
  Aurophobia [fear of gold]

- Irrational fear/hatred usually exhibited by people when politicians talk about the need to find a balance between freedom and security
  Automatonophobia [fear of ventriloquist's dummies]

- Irrational fear/hatred usually exhibited by people when they shake hands with someone who has just been to the bathroom

Automysophobia [fear of being dirty]

- **Irrational fear/hatred usually exhibited by sharks after they catch a puffer fish**
  Belonephobia [fear of needles or sharp objects]

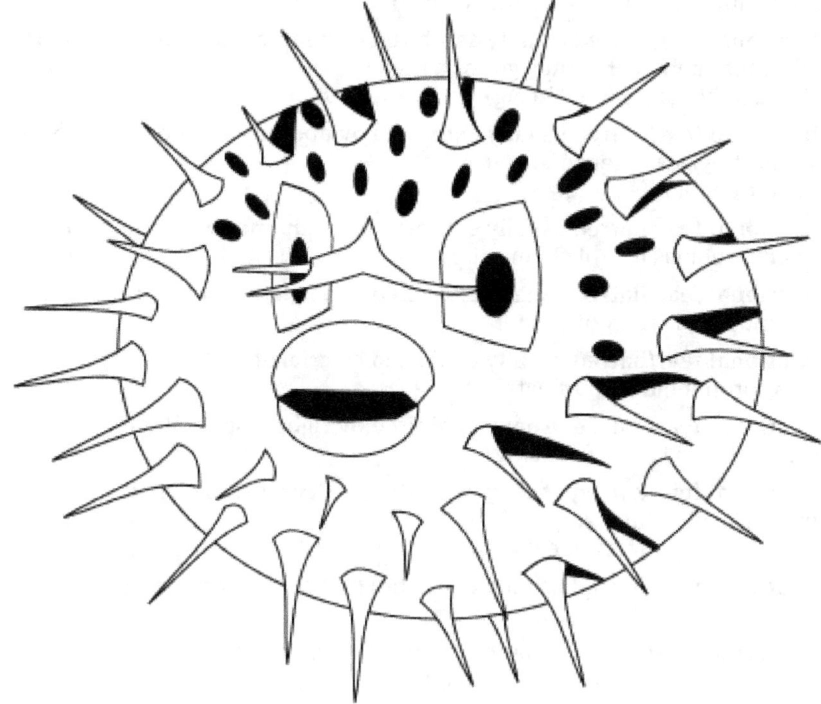

- **Irrational fear/hatred exhibited by door handles of public bathrooms**
  Bacteriophobia [fear of bacteria]

- **Irrational fear/hatred usually exhibited by people when they encounter drunkards**
  Batrachophobia [fear of amphibians]

- **Irrational fear/hatred usually exhibited people when they tumble down the stairs during a power cut**
  Bathophobia [fear of depth]

- **Irrational obsession usually exhibited by silverfish**
  Bibliomania [love of books]

- **Irrational fear/hatred usually exhibited by the public when dealing with corrupt government officials**
  Blennophobia [fear of slime]

- **Irrational fear/hatred usually exhibited by teenagers**
  Cacophobia [fear of ugliness]

- **Irrational fear/hatred usually exhibited by opponents of mobile phone radiation**
  Carcinophobia [fear of cancer]

- **Irrational fear/hatred usually exhibited by Count Dracula, Nosferatu, and**

other vampires
Catoptrophobia [fear of mirrors]

- **Irrational fear/hatred usually exhibited by male mosquitoes when they tell other insects that it is the females of their species that drink blood**
Catagelophobia [fear of being ridiculed]

- **Irrational fear/hatred usually exhibited by people when they think others will take their seat if they go for a break**
Cathisophobia [fear of sitting]

- **Irrational fear/hatred usually exhibited by operators of heavy machinery when they get dragged into it**
Chaetophobia [fear of hair]

- **Irrational fear/hatred usually exhibited by proponents of organic foods**
Chemophobia [fear of chemicals]

- **Irrational fear/hatred usually exhibited by Christmas trees**
Chionophobia [fear of snow]

- **Irrational fear/hatred usually exhibited by cricket balls**
Chiroptophobia [fear of bats]

- **Irrational fear/hatred usually exhibited by tight-rope walkers**
Chorophobia [fear of dancing]

- **Irrational fear/hatred usually exhibited by dry cleaners when they are washing all-whites**
Chromophobia [fear of colours]

- **Irrational fear/hatred usually exhibited by people living in the past**
Chronophobia [fear of time]

- **Irrational fear/hatred usually exhibited by procrastinators**
Chronomentrophobia [fear of clocks]

- **Irrational fear/hatred usually exhibited by fashion models**
Cibophobia [fear of food]

- **Irrational fear/hatred usually exhibited by protesters and jail inmates**
Claustrophobia [fear of enclosed spaces]

- **Irrational fear/hatred usually exhibited by movers-and-packers**
Climacophobia [fear of stairs]

- **Irrational fear/hatred usually exhibited by kids after they watch a horror movie**
Clinophobia [fear of going to bed]

- **Irrational fear/hatred usually exhibited by people disgusted with politics**
Coulrophobia [fear of clowns]

- **Irrational fear/hatred usually exhibited by people after they accidentally format the hard disk**
Cyberphobia [fear of computers]

- **Irrational fear/hatred usually exhibited by people when they take a seat and fail to note the Chihuahua on it**
Cynophobia [fear of dogs]

- **Irrational fear/hatred usually exhibited by zombies when they wake up and become hungry again**

Coimetrophobia [fear of cemeteries]

- **Irrational fear/hatred usually exhibited by formerly possessed individuals when they clean their room after an exorcism**
  Demonophobia [fear of demons]

- **Irrational fear/hatred usually exhibited by horse-riders when they get stopped by a branch**
  Dendrophobia [fear of trees]

- **Irrational fear/hatred usually exhibited by people during earthquakes**
  Domatophobia [fear of houses]

- **Irrational fear/hatred usually exhibited by fish when approaching a group of sharks**
  Didaskaleinophobia [fear of going to school]

- **Irrational fear/hatred usually exhibited by people when they fall from a cliff while taking a selfie**
  Dinophobia [fear of dizziness]

- **Irrational fear/hatred usually exhibited by vampires after biting a Russian**
  Dipsophobia [fear of alcohol]

- **Irrational desire that a policeman with a breathalyser would like in passing motorists**
  Dipsomania [love of alcohol]

- **Irrational fear/hatred usually exhibited by sheep when they spot a wolf in disguise amidst them**
  Doraphobia [fear of fur or hide of animals]

- **Irrational fear/hatred usually exhibited by ants when they are transporting stuff to great heights**

Dystychiphobia [fear of accidents]

- **Irrational fear/hatred usually exhibited by spies**
  Dysmorphophobia [fear of body flaws]

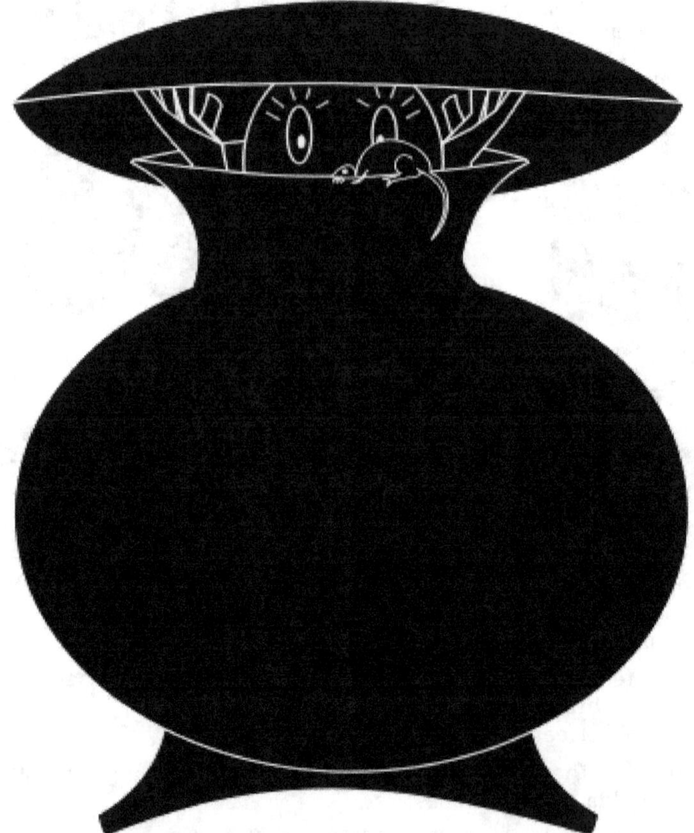

- **Irrational fear/hatred usually exhibited by formerly possessed individuals when they receive the bill from the exorcist**
  Ecclesiophobia [fear of church]

- **Irrational fear/hatred usually lacking in birds when they sit on power cables**
  Irrational fear/hatred usually exhibited by people when the drop the phone extension cord in the bathtub
  Irrational fear/hatred usually exhibited by women when the drop the hair dryer in the bathtub
  Electrophobia [fear of electricity]

- **Irrational fear/hatred usually exhibited by skydivers when their parachute fails to deploy**
  Eleutherophobia [fear of freedom]

- **Irrational fear/hatred usually exhibited by visitors to an acupuncturist's clinic when they fall to the floor**
  Enetophobia [fear of pins]

- **Irrational fear/hatred usually exhibited by unpopular politicians and police**

states
Enochlophobia [fear of crowds]

- **Irrational fear/hatred usually exhibited by people who hate Mondays**
Eosophobia [fear of daylight]

- **Irrational fear/hatred usually exhibited by walls disfigured by graffiti**
Ephebiphobia [fear of youth]

- **Irrational fear/hatred usually exhibited by pugilists when their eyelids swell up**
Epistaxiophobia [fear of nosebleeds]

- **Irrational fear/hatred usually exhibited by whistleblowers when a hitman pays a visit**
Epistemophobia [fear of knowledge]

- **Irrational fear/hatred usually exhibited by mules when they get ridiculed for looking like a donkey**
Equinophobia [fear of horses]

- **Irrational fear/hatred usually lacking in pension funds**
Erythrophobia [fear of the colour red]

- **Irrational fear/hatred usually exhibited by condemned prisoners when they reach the guillotine**
Francophobia [fear of France or French culture]

- **Irrational fear/hatred usually exhibited by homeless people and stray animals at night**
Frigophobia [fear of cold]

- **Irrational fear/hatred usually exhibited by divorce lawyers when marriage statistics indicate that relationships are lasting longer**
Gamophobia [fear of marriage]

- **Irrational fear/hatred usually exhibited by lionesses when they abandon their kill to hyenas**
Gelotophobia [fear of laughter]

- **Irrational fear/hatred usually exhibited comedians when their jokes are stolen**
Gelotophobia [fear of being laughed at]

- **Irrational fear/hatred usually exhibited by boatmen**
Gephyrophobia [fear of bridges]

- **Irrational fear/hatred usually exhibited by suicide bombers**
Gerascophobia [fear of growing old]

- **Irrational fear/hatred usually exhibited by kids when they are caught with their hands in the cookie jar**
Gerontophobia [fear of the elderly]

- **Irrational fear/hatred usually exhibited by victims of blimp crashes**
Globophobia [fear of balloons]

- **Irrational fear/hatred usually exhibited by politicians when the teleprompter fails**
Glossophobia [fear of public speaking]

- **Irrational fear/hatred usually exhibited by people when they cannot**

understand their own notes
Graphophobia [fear of handwriting]

- **Irrational fear/hatred usually exhibited by taxmen when they approach the last date for their return to the ungodly place they came from**
Hadephobia [fear of hell]

- **Irrational fear/hatred usually exhibited by vampires when the exorcist throws The Book at them**
Hagiophobia [fear of holy/sacred things]

- **Irrational fear/hatred usually exhibited by a lizard after it catches a stink bug by mistake**
Halitophobia [fear of bad breath]

- **Irrational fear/hatred usually exhibited by people who take the last biscuit without first offering it to others**
Hamartophobia [fear of sinning]

- **Irrational fear/hatred usually exhibited by athletes when a rival uses crooked ways to win**
Harpaxophobia [fear of being robbed]

- **Irrational fear/hatred usually exhibited by a death row inmate before his/her last meal**
Hedonophobia [fear of pleasure]

- **Irrational fear/hatred usually exhibited by vampires**
Heliophobia [fear of sunlight]

- **Irrational fear/hatred usually exhibited by businesses when they pay huge fines in class-action lawsuits**
Hellenologophobia [fear of complex terminology]

- **Irrational fear/hatred usually exhibited by computer antivirus companies**
Helminthophobia [fear of worms]

- **Irrational fear/hatred usually exhibited by hæmophiliacs**
Hemophobia [fear of blood]

- **Irrational fear/hatred usually exhibited by party officials when a politician deviates from talking points**
Heresyphobia [fear of heresy]

- **Irrational fear/hatred usually exhibited by Japanese people when Godzilla makes landfall**
Herpetophobia [fear of reptiles]

- **Irrational fear/hatred usually exhibited by boys when they get ragged in front of female students of their class**
Heterophobia [fear of opposite gender]

- **Irrational fear/hatred of a particular number sometimes exhibited by people who are afraid of the number 999**
Hexakosioihexekontahexaphobia [fear of the number 666]

- **Irrational fear/hatred of usually exhibited by people when they have to admit their mistake**
Hippopotomonstrosesquipedaliophobia [fear of long words]

- **Irrational fear/hatred usually exhibited by societies that fail to take care of their own brethren**

Hobophobia [fear of hobos]

- **Irrational fear/hatred usually exhibited by statues**
  Hodophobia [fear of travel]
- **Irrational fear/hatred usually exhibited by passive smokers**
  Homichlophobia [fear of fog]
- **Irrational fear/hatred usually exhibited by men when they get teary-eyed while watching a sad cartoon**
  Hygrophobia [fear of dampness]

- **Irrational fear/hatred usually exhibited by kids after they break something expensive**
  Homilophobia [fear of sermons]
- **Irrational fear/hatred usually exhibited by kids when they do not get a bigger slice than their younger sibling**
  Homophobia [fear of sameness]
- **Irrational fear/hatred usually exhibited by gun owners when they shoot themselves in the leg**
  Hoplophobia [fear of firearms]
- **Irrational fear/hatred usually exhibited by women after they drop the hair dryer in the bathtub**
  Hormephobia [fear of shocks]
- **Irrational fear/hatred which explains why Batman is still single**
  Hydrophobophobia [fear of rabies]
- **Irrational fear/hatred usually exhibited by insects**
  Hyelophobia [fear of glasses]
- **Irrational fear/hatred usually exhibited by people when someone calls them names that accurately describe them**
  Hylephobia [fear of fits or epilepsy]
- **Irrational fear/hatred usually exhibited by people when they fail to shave**

Hylophobia [fear of forests]

- **Irrational fear/hatred usually exhibited by kids when their siblings rat on them**
  Hypengyophobia [fear of responsibility]

- **Irrational fear/hatred usually exhibited by people when a politician talks about his accomplishments**
  Hypnophobia [fear of sleep]

- **Irrational fear/hatred usually exhibited by smokers when their lungs have accumulated enough tar to top the driveway where the hearse is waiting to pick them up**
  Hypochondria [fear of illness]

- **Irrational fear/hatred usually exhibited by people when they know they are going to be hit with a huge bill**
  Iatrophobia [fear of doctors or visiting them]

- **Irrational fear/hatred usually exhibited by debtors when a package arrives without any postage marks**
  Ichthyophobia [fear of fish]

- **Irrational fear/hatred usually exhibited by many politicians**
  Ideophobia [fear of ideas]

- **Irrational fear/hatred usually exhibited by speculators when the bubble bursts**
  Illyngophobia [fear of vertigo]

- **Irrational fear/hatred usually exhibited by the public when bureaucrats and politicians divert scarce public resources to white-elephant projects**
  Isopterophobia [fear of termites]

- **Irrational desire usually exhibited by many politicians when they are in power**
  Kleptomania [love of stealing or stolen goods]

- **Irrational fear/hatred usually exhibited by restaurant owners during a food-and-health inspection**
  Katsaridaphobia [fear of cockroaches]

- **Irrational fear/hatred usually exhibited by the public when they try to explain their problems to a politician or government official**
  Kenophobia [fear of empty spaces]

- **Irrational fear/hatred usually exhibited by demolition experts**
  Koinoniphobia [fear of rooms]

- **Irrational fear/hatred usually exhibited by someone who catches a tiger by its tail**
  Kopophobia [fear of fatigue]

- **Irrational fear/hatred usually exhibited by an opera singer when a mobile phone rings loudly during a performance**
  Kymophobia [fear of waves]

- **Irrational fear/hatred usually exhibited by people when politicians prove to be spineless**
  Kyphophobia [fear of stooping]

- **Irrational fear/hatred usually exhibited by kids when mother cooks bitter**

gourd because it is rich in minerals
Lachanophobia [fear of vegetables]

- **Irrational fear/hatred usually exhibited by a Mafia leader when a gang member sings like a canary**
Laliophobia [fear of speaking]

- **Irrational fear/hatred usually exhibited by people who spend too much time on the keyboard**
Leprophobia [fear of leprosy]

- **Irrational fear/hatred usually exhibited by a terrorist when he throws the pin and bites the grenade**
Ligyrophobia [fear of loud noises]

- **Irrational fear/hatred usually exhibited by fairies, billboards and men-on-stilts**
Lilapsophobia [fear of tornadoes/hurricanes]

- **Irrational fear/hatred usually exhibited by whistleblowers**
Limnophobia [fear of lakes]

- **Irrational fear/hatred usually exhibited by liars**
Linonophobia [fear of string]

- **Irrational fear/hatred usually exhibited by a hungry vampire when it ignores an American**
Liticaphobia [fear of lawsuits]

- **Irrational fear/hatred usually exhibited by Morse code operators**
Logophobia [fear of words]

- **Irrational fear/hatred usually exhibited by kids when mother takes forever to get the icecream after meals**
Macrophobia [fear of long waits]

- **Irrational fear/hatred usually exhibited by spiders, lizards, insects and other creatures that live in the kitchen**
Mageirocophobia [fear of cooking]

- **Irrational fear/hatred usually lacking in government officials**
Mastigophobia [fear of punishment]

- **Irrational fear/hatred usually exhibited by fruits when they go into the blender**
Mechanophobia [fear of machines]

- **Irrational fear/hatred usually exhibited by people when they find a few spots on fruits and vegetables forcing stores to waste good food prematurely**
Melanophobia [fear of black colour]

- **Irrational fear/hatred usually exhibited by drones when the workers come for the evening**
Melissophobia [fear of bees]

- **Irrational fear/hatred usually exhibited by teenagers after they wreck the family car**
Melophobia [fear of music]

- **Irrational fear/hatred usually exhibited by a jail inmate who has been sentenced to hang**

Merinthophobia [fear of being tied up]

- **Irrational fear/hatred usually exhibited by MRI operators when someone rolls in an oxygen tank**
  Metallophobia [fear of metal]

- **Irrational fear/hatred usually exhibited by parents when their kids scribbles on the wall**
  Metrophobia [fear of poems]

- **Irrational fear/hatred usually sometimes exhibited by kids when everyone else escapes punishment**
  Monophobia [fear of being alone]

- **Irrational fear/hatred usually exhibited by parking area attendants**
  Motorphobia [fear of automobiles]

- **Irrational fear/hatred usually exhibited by lizards when the dust gets into their eyes**
  Mottephobia [fear of moths]

- **Irrational fear/hatred usually exhibited by snakes when they learn that health authorities have declared the area plague-affected**
  Murophobia [fear of mice and rats]

- **Irrational fear/hatred usually lacking in people when they are praised**
  Myrmecophobia [fear of ants]

- **Irrational compulsion felt by politicians when they state their accomplishments**
  Mythomania [love of lying]

- **Irrational fear/hatred usually exhibited by canned food**
  Mysophobia [fear of germs or contamination]

- **Irrational fear/hatred usually exhibited by torches when the light goes dim**
  Necrophobia [fear of death or the dead]

- **Irrational fear/hatred (according to feminists) usually exhibited by women when they throw a brick at the ceiling**
  Nelophobia [fear of glass]

- **Irrational fear/hatred usually exhibited by a blockbuster drug manufacturer when a generic equivalent enters the market**
  Neopharmaphobia [fear of new drugs]

- **Irrational fear/hatred usually exhibited by an overdue sacrificial goat when fresh arrivals join the lot**
  Neophobia [fear of new things]

- **Irrational fear/hatred usually exhibited by somnabulists living in a landmined area**
  Noctiphobia [fear of the night]

- **Irrational fear/hatred usually exhibited by horror movie actors when the ghost deploys a cell phone jammer**
  Nomophobia [fear of lack of mobile phone service]

- **Irrational fear/hatred usually exhibited by footboard travellers when they start slipping**
  Nosocomephobia [fear of hospitals]

- **Irrational fear/hatred usually exhibited by surgical gloves**
  Nosophobia [fear of diseases]

- **Irrational fear/hatred usually exhibited by bomb-disposal squad members**
  Numerophobia [fear of numbers]

- **Irrational fear/hatred usually exhibited by horror movie actors when they realize it was a mistake to have split up and gone in different directions**
  Nyctohylophobia [fear of forested areas at night]

- **Irrational fear/hatred usually exhibited by American turkeys ahead of Thanksgiving**
  Obesophobia [fear of weight gain]

- **Irrational fear/hatred usually exhibited by missionaries caught by a cannibal tribe**
  Ochlophobia [fear of crowds]

- **Irrational fear/hatred usually exhibited by candy-loving kids**
  Odontophobia [fear of dentistry]

- **Irrational fear/hatred usually exhibited by parade organizers**
  Ombrophobia [fear of rain]

- **Irrational fear/hatred usually exhibited by pickpockets**
  Ommetaphobia [fear of eyes]

- **Irrational fear/hatred that Adam and Eve were unlikely to have**
  Omphalophobia [fear of belly button]

- **Irrational fear/hatred usually exhibited by Indians when they try to navigate the bureaucracy**
  Oneirophobia [fear of dreams]

- **Irrational obsession usually exhibited by authoritarian states when they try to extract truth from suspects and troublemakers**
  Onychotillomania [love of picking fingernails]

- **Irrational fear/hatred exhibited by tourists in tropical South America when they fall into anaconda-infested waters**
  Ophidiophobia [fear of snakes]

- **Irrational fear/hatred usually exhibited around people with looks that can kill**
  Ophthalmophobia [fear of staring]

- **Irrational fear/hatred exhibited by people when they sneeze**
  Optophobia [fear of opening one's eyes]

- **Irrational fear/hatred usually exhibited by statues**
  Ornithophobia [fear of birds]

- **Irrational fear/hatred usually exhibited by psychopaths when power fails to return and the bodies in the freezer are losing their cool**
  Osmophobia [fear of odours]

- **Irrational fear/hatred usually exhibited by pearl divers when they get trapped inside a clam**
  Ostraconophobia [fear of shellfish]

- **Irrational fear/hatred usually exhibited by people hit by lightning**
  Ouranophobia [fear of heaven]

- **Irrational fear/hatred usually exhibited by people after they stick their tongue to a metal pole**
  Pagophobia [fear of ice or frost]

- **Irrational fear/hatred usually exhibited by drug cartel members when they seek to settle all deals in cash**
  Papyrophobia [fear of paper]

- **Irrational fear/hatred usually exhibited by politicians when they get admitted to hospital while their lawyer tries to arrange for bail**
  Panphobia [fear of everything and/or unknown stuff]

- **Irrational fear/hatred usually exhibited by taxpayers**
  Parasitophobia [fear of parasites]

- **Irrational fear/hatred usually exhibited by taxmen when they are dipped in boiling oil in hell**
  Peccatophobia [fear of sinning]

- **Irrational fear/hatred usually exhibited by head-hunters**
  Pediculophobia [fear of lice]

- **Irrational fear/hatred usually exhibited by voodoo practitioners when the tax department sends them an unsolicited, skewered and crude likeness by registered mail**
  Pediophobia [fear of dolls]

- **Irrational fear/hatred usually exhibited by hair oil manufacturers**
  Peladophobia [fear of bald people]

- **Irrational fear/hatred usually exhibited by burglars**
  Peniaphobia [fear of poverty]

- **Irrational fear/hatred usually exhibited by a male praying mantis**
  Peniaphobia [fear of mother-in-law]
- **Irrational fear/hatred usually exhibited by the public when they think of the tax being collected by the government**
  Irrational fear/hatred usually exhibited by forest explorers when a python gets a crush on them
  Phagophobia [fear of being eaten]
- **Irrational fear/hatred that was usually exhibited by early American settlers when they saw Red Indians with tomahawks eyeing their scalp**
  Phalacrophobia [fear of going bald]
- **Irrational fear/hatred usually exhibited by people when the cure is worse than the disease**
  Pharmacophobia [fear of medicines]
- **Irrational fear/hatred usually exhibited by politicians when opponents dig up their past**
  Phasmophobia [fear of ghosts]
- **Irrational desire usually exhibited by people when they note the overbite problem of a vampire for the first time**
  Philematophobia [fear of kissing]
- **Irrational desire usually exhibited by frogs when they encounter snakes**
  Philophobia [fear of love]
- **Irrational fear/hatred usually exhibited by people when someone says "I told you so"**
  Philosophobia [fear of philosophy]
- **Irrational fear/hatred usually exhibited by a zombie when it tries to get out**
  Placophobia [fear of tombstones]

- **Irrational fear/hatred usually exhibited by people who do not have enough problems**
  Phobophobia [fear of phobias]
- **Irrational fear/hatred usually exhibited by tobacco products**

Photophobia [fear of light]

- **Irrational fear/hatred usually exhibited by barbers**
  Pogonophobia [fear of beards]

- **Irrational fear/hatred usually exhibited by politicians when "high command" gives their "lucrative posts" to fresh arrivals from rival political parties**
  Politicophobia [fear of politicians]

- **Irrational fear/hatred usually exhibited by scared folk who are also egomaniacs**
  Polyphobia [fear of many things]

- **Irrational fear/hatred usually exhibited by taxmen**
  Plutophobia [fear of wealth]

- **Irrational fear/hatred usually exhibited by Chihuahuas owned by sumo wrestlers**
  Pnigophobia [fear of being smothered]

- **Irrational fear/hatred usually exhibited by lawyers when cases seem to end fast**
  Prosophobia [fear of progress]

- **Irrational fear/hatred usually exhibited by people when they have to manufacture a lie and say it at the same time**
  Psellismophobia [fear of stuttering]

- **Irrational fear/hatred usually exhibited by trapeze artists**
  Pteronophobia [fear of being tickled by feathers]

- **Irrational desire usually exhibited by Indians around the festival of Diwali**
  Pyromania [love of fire]

- **Irrational fear/hatred usually exhibited by a soldier when he is cleaning a cannon from the business end and hears an order followed by some light at the end of the tunnel**
  Pyrophobia [fear of fire]

- **Irrational fear/hatred usually exhibited by dragonflies when they buzz over water bodies**
  Ranidaphobia [fear of frogs]

- **Irrational fear/hatred usually exhibited by terrorists**
  Radiophobia [fear of x-rays or radioactivity]

- **Irrational fear/hatred usually exhibited by tourists in Russia when try to out-drink the hosts**
  Russophobia [fear of Russians]

- **Irrational fear/hatred usually exhibited by horror movie actors**
  Sciophobia [fear of shadows]

- **Irrational fear/hatred usually exhibited by gamblers when they borrow money they cannot pay and hear a knock on the door**
  Selachophobia [fear of sharks]

- **Irrational fear/hatred usually exhibited by werewolves when dog food prices rise**
  Selenophobia [fear of the moon]

- **Irrational fear/hatred usually exhibited by models when they have to pose for photos without payment**
  Scopophobia [fear of being looked at]

- **Irrational fear/hatred usually lacking in many people with selfie sticks**
  Siderodromophobia [fear of trains]

- **Irrational fear/hatred usually exhibited by people when they walk into a curtain and hit their head on the edge of a door**
  Siderophobia [fear of stars]

- **Irrational fear/hatred usually exhibited by people when they buy a product and realise that the instructions are in a foreign language**
  Sinophobia [fear of Chinese]

- **Irrational fear/hatred usually exhibited by burglars**
  Sociophobia [fear of people and social interactions]

- **Irrational fear/hatred usually exhibited by women when they realize it is their birthday**
  Sophophobia [fear of learning]

- **Irrational fear/hatred usually exhibited by the person who climbs to the top of a human pyramid**
  Soteriophobia [fear of dependence on others]

- **Irrational fear/hatred usually exhibited by sofa manufacturers**
  Stasiphobia [fear of standing]

- **Irrational fear/hatred usually exhibited by owls when it realizes that its slow quarry was poisoned**
  Suriphobia [fear of mice]
  [Poisoned vermin should be incinerated.]

- **Irrational fear/hatred usually exhibited by caterers when the queue forms**
  Tachophobia [fear of speed]

- **Irrational fear/hatred usually exhibited by ants around beachball players**
  Taphophobia [fear of being buried alive]

- **Irrational fear/hatred usually exhibited by horror movie actors when they run away from zombies**
  Teratophobia [fear of disfigured people]

- **Irrational fear/hatred usually exhibited by people sitting on a 3-seat bench in a very crowded train**
  Tetraphobia [fear of number 4]

- **Irrational fear/hatred usually exhibited by a chain mail when it meets a sceptic**
  Thanatophobia [fear of dying]

- **Irrational fear/hatred usually exhibited by mobsters when their feet gets stuck in a tub full of concrete**
  Thalassophobia [fear of sea]

- **Irrational fear/hatred usually exhibited by missionaries when they convert natives**
  Theophobia [fear of religion]

- **Irrational fear/hatred usually exhibited by acupuncturists during an earthquake**

Tremophobia [fear of trembling]

- **Irrational fear/hatred usually exhibited by icecream containers**
Thermophobia [fear of high temperatures]

- **Irrational fear/hatred usually exhibited by a kid worried about sharing his/her toys with a future sibling**
Tokophobia [fear of pregnancy or childbirth]

- **Irrational fear/hatred usually exhibited by people living in border areas**
Tomophobia [fear of invasive medical procedures]

- **Irrational fear/hatred usually exhibited by movies in which all top-secret government computers run PowerPoint 1.0 for DOS and no other software**

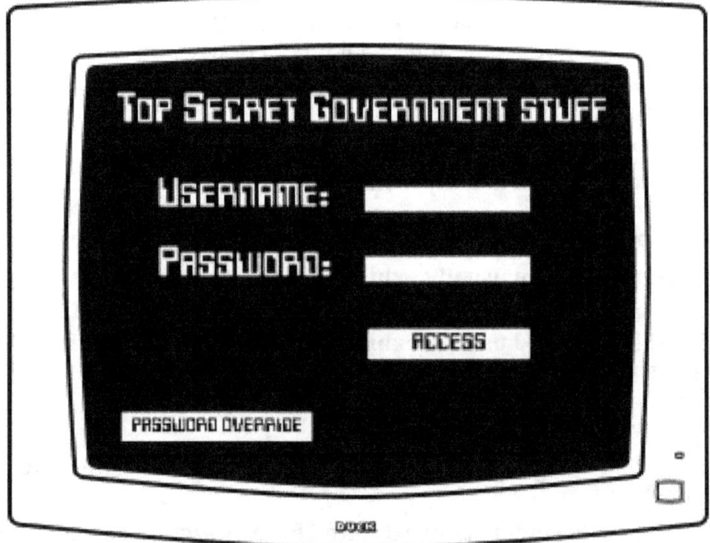

Technophobia [fear of advanced technology]

- **Irrational fear/hatred usually exhibited by a snake when it bites its tongue**
Toxiphobia [fear of poisoning]

- **Irrational fear/hatred usually exhibited by parkour enthusiasts when they can not move their body**
Traumatophobia [fear of trauma or injury]

- **Irrational love/desire usually exhibited by people when the election results are announced**
Trichotillomania [love of plucking hair]

- **Irrational desire usually exhibited by pre-teen kids when they realize that soon they will have to do a lot more household chores like their older siblings**
Triskaidekaphobia [fear of number 13]

- **Irrational fear/hatred usually exhibited by people when they realize that a mosquito is biting them**
Trypanophobia [fear of needles]

- **Irrational fear/hatred usually exhibited by those engaged in gun fights**

Trypophobia [fear of holes]

- **Irrational fear/hatred usually exhibited by kids when someone with a new bat lords it over everyone**
  Tyrannophobia [fear of tyrants]
- **Irrational fear/hatred usually exhibited by beautiful women when they encounter women more beautiful than them**
  Venustraphobia [fear of beautiful women]
- **Irrational fear/hatred usually exhibited by men when women do the packing**
  Vestiphobia [fear of clothing]
- **Irrational fear/hatred usually exhibited by teenagers when someone tries to talk sense to them**
  Xenoglossophobia [fear of foreign languages]
- **Irrational fear/hatred usually exhibited by people when their shoe comes apart in the middle of the street**
  Xenophobia [fear of strangers or aliens]
- **Irrational fear/hatred usually exhibited by desks when the judge raises the gavel**
  Xylophobia [fear of wooden objects]
- **Irrational fear/hatred usually exhibited by librarians**
  Xyrophobia [fear of razors]
- **Irrational fear/hatred usually exhibited by kids when they realize that their sibling still has not finished his/her candy**
  Zelophobia [fear of jealousy]
- **Irrational fear/hatred usually exhibited by alcoholics when they quit drinking after doctors tells them they have cirrhosis**
  Zeusophobia [fear of god]
  [WARNING: Sudden cessation of alcohol without medical supervision will also cause problems.]
- **Irrational fear/hatred usually exhibited by vegans/vegetarians**
  Zoophobia [fear of animals]

Knock-Knock Jokes

Knock-knock jokes are best enjoyed with two or more people. They are enacted as a scene in which a stranger is seeking entry in to a restricted area. The person who knows the joke acts as the stranger and begins by saying "Knock knock". Somebody in the audience pretends to be the guard and has to say, "Who goes there?". Then, the stranger says a word (usually his/her name) that is the subject of the joke. The guard replies to that with "

- **Arthur**

  Knock Knock.
  Who is there?
  Arthur.
  Arthur who?
  Are there any back taxes you owe?

- **Bill**

  Knock Knock.
  Who is there?
  Bill.
  Bill who?
  Believe it or not, your car is being towed.

- **Cedric**

  Knock Knock.
  Who is there?
  Cedric.
  Cedric who?
  See, the trick is to close the windows as well. You're letting the mosquitoes in.

- **Dees**

  Knock Knock.
  Who is there?
  Dees.
  Dees who?
  Dees eez the poleez!

- **Emmy**

  Knock Knock.
  Who is there?
  Emmy.
  Emmy who?
  Emm I interrupting you?

- **Fredrick**

  Knock Knock.
  Who is there?
  Fredrick.
  Fredrick who?
  For the record, it's Fredrick with a K.

- **Gee**

  Knock Knock.
  Who is there?
  Giselle.
  Giselle who?
  Gee, I shall bring the gin.

- **Humour**

  Knock Knock.
  Who is there?
  Humour.
  Humour who?
  No, Yuma, Colorado.

- **Isla**

  Knock Knock.
  Who is there?
  Isla.
  Isla who?
  I'd love to come in!

- **Johnny**

  Knock Knock.
  Who is there?
  Johnny.
  Johnny who?
  Johnny come lately!

- **Kenny**

  Knock Knock.
  Who is there?
  Kenny.
  Kenny who?
  Can I know your name?

- **Luke**

  Knock Knock.
  Who is there?
  Luke.
  Luke who?
  Look, who is coming to dinner.

- **Meg**

  Knock Knock.
  Who is there?
  Meg.
  Meg who?
  Make haste. It is cold outside!

- **Naomi**

  Knock Knock.
  Who is there?
  It's Naomi.
  Naomi who?
  Nah, you owe me a dollar!

- **Ooma**

  Knock Knock.
  Who is there?
  It's Ooma.
  Ooma who?
  Who am I talking to?

- **Police**

  Knock Knock.
  Who is there?
  Police.
  Police who?
  Puhlease, it's an emergency!

- **Queen**

  Knock Knock.
  Who is there?
  Queen.
  Queen who?
  Go in and get my coat! It's raining.

- **Rhonda**

  Knock Knock.
  Who is there?
  Rhonda.
  Rhonda who?
  Run, da police are here.

- **Tom**

  Knock Knock.
  Who is there?
  Tom.
  Tom who?
  To whom... say, your name is what?

- **Uranus**

  Knock Knock.
  Who is there?
  Uranus.
  What?
  Uranus!
  Uranus, the planet?
  No, it's *Your Highness* who will have you executed if you don't open the door!

- **Wikipedia**

  Knock Knock.
  Who is there?
  Wikipedia
  Wikipedia who?
  Wikipedia, the free online encyclopedia that anybody can edit!
  [citation needed]

- **Wilma**

Knock Knock.
Who is there?
Wilma
Wilma who?
Will my beautiful woman come to the door and open it, please?

- **Xavier**

Knock Knock.
Who is there?
Xavier
Xavier who?
Save your talk. You have the right to remain silent.

- **Yvonne**

Knock Knock.
Who is there?
Yvonne
Yvonne who?
You own this house? Your property taxes are due.

- **Zohra**

Knock Knock.
Who is there?
Zohra
Zohra who?
Sir, are you the owner of this house?

- **Opportunity**

Knock.
Who is there?
Opportunity.
Opportunity who?
[Silence]

... because opportunity knocks only once.

Mix Jokes

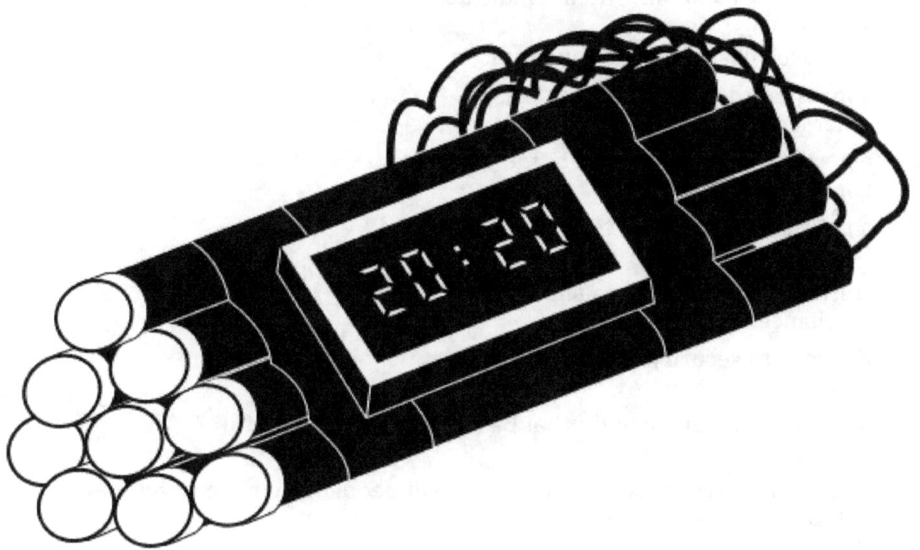

Each question in this section begins with "What do you get when you cross...".

- **an elk from New York and a character?**
  Anonymous letter.

- **a good-looking woman and sunshine?**
  Broad daylight.

- **a female with an AC remote?**
  Very rapid, unexplained, woman-made Climate Change.

- **a precious stone and a fast bowler?**
  Not a *diamond in the rough*.

- **a smart chicken and shy rooster**
  Scrambled eggs.

- **a financial magazine with a bank employee?**
  Fortune teller.

- **an old lady and epilepsy?**
  Grand mal seizure.

- **incorruptibility with an Indian policeman?**
  Hell freezes over.

- **whisky and a draught animal?**
  High horse.

- ***India Today* magazine with *Reader's Digest*?**
  Indigestion Today.

- **an unknown man with a female deer?**
  John Doe.

- **an unknown woman with a female deer?**
  - Jane Doe.
  - Broken chain of gossip and rumour.

- **a mass murder with a binocular?**
  Killer looks.

- **a grandfather clock with a burqa?**
  Long time no see.

- **a politician and a high tolerance for praise?**
  Made for each other.

- **truthfulness and a bureaucrat?**
  No chance.

- **rights with security?**
  Orwellian times.

- **a talking head and a brain that has never been used before?**
  Politician.

- **free food and the fastest thing a group of people who have never met before can do together?**
  Queue.

- **a kid and a holiday wishlist?**
  Reasonable expectations.

- **an alarm clock and a bomb?**
  Time killer.

- **talcum powder and a surgeon?**
  Smooth operator.

- **film director Quentin Tarantino and a mathematical procedure?**
  Tarantula.

- **a meaningless pause, the European pre-Christian god of thunder and a dude?**
  Uma Thurman, the actress.

- **modesty with a politician?**
  You are nuts.

- **efficiency with a government official?**
  Zero likelihood.

Physics Jokes

Science was my favourite subject in school. Physics was an easy subject until I reached higher secondary school. Then, it became difficult. That is, until I found the Feynman Lectures On Physics in the school library. After reading it, the physics textbook became easy to understand. Unfortunately, much of the year had passed and I could not put the book to good use for my final exam. If you choose physics as an elective subject, get Feynman's first.

- **Personal Ad**
  Invisible Man wants to meet wholesome invisible woman with transparent character and zero refraction.

- **Personal Ad**
  Invisible Woman wants to meet handsome invisible man with strong character and no infractions.

- **Perfect Chemistry**
  Invisible Man wanted to marry Invisible Woman. His family and friends did not like the idea. They could not figure out what he saw in her.

- **Science Fiction?**
  The Invisible Man* by HG Wells became so popular that the original magazine series was converted into a book and later adapted into several movies and TV shows. It continues to capture the imagination of young and old. However, is it really science fiction? Can someone become invisible? Let us assume that it is possible. How will this person be? Well, for one thing, he will have to be dead.

To let light through, the molecules in the body will have to be aligned like a lattice as in a crystal. No fluids (liquids or gas) could be present as they would have different densities and could be seen sloshing around. The colour of a material is directly related to its chemical composition. In what combination of chemicals can the human body become transparent? Can it stay alive? Even assuming that it can, **Invisible Man will have to be blind**, as his eyes will not be able to reflect light and form an image for the brain.

The technology to create an invisibility cloak effect has been in existence for several decades now. It is used in battlefields to camouflage tanks. These vehicles carry flat displays on top of them, which mimic the ground underneath to create the illusion that they are not really there (when observed from the sky). Such invisibility cloaks are available for military personnel and fixed installations too.

- **Pluto walks into a bar**
  Pluto walks into a bar but the bartender ignores him. Why? Because nobody recognizes Pluto as a planet anymore.

- **A meteor asks a meteorite**
  A meteor asks a meteorite, "What are my chances of hitting the ground?" The meteorite does not answer and just smiles. Irritated, the meteor says, "Aah, you guys just burn me up!"

- **How many astronauts would it take to a screw a lightbulb?**
  One to turn the bulb and several to prevent the spacecraft from spinning in the same direction.

- **What did one radio wave say to another?**
  "You are interfering with my work."

- **What's a radio engineer's favourite food?**
  A can of tuna.

- **What would happen if an eel came on the radio?**
  - You hear loud static once in a while.
  - "You are listening to *Current Affairs*, a programme about events that are electrifying the political arena."

- **What does Galileo's school yearbook say about him?**
  "Most likely to get arrested for using a telescope."

- **What was the crocodile searching on the Internet?**
  Alligator clips.

This is an electronics joke.

- **What would happen if lightning was elected mayor?**
  It would be illegal to steal someone's thunder.

- **What did the battery say to the circuit?**
  "If you lose my charge, you are grounded."

- **What did one equation say to another?**
  "What's with the odd expression?"

- **What happened when lead was dropped in water?**
  It had that sinking feeling.

- **Why did the physicist couple break up?**

They could not handle the pressure.

- **What did the quantum gas think of Absolute Zero?**
  It was not very excited.

- **What did 10^{-12} say to 10^{-9}?**
  "Pico on somebody else!"

- **What did 10^{-9} say to make 10^{-6} so angry?**
  "Nano of your business!"

- **What do protons like to read?**
  Books like "The power of positive thinking".

- **What did the neutron say when it was arrested?**
  "What's the charge?"

- **A proton walks into a bar**
  A proton walks into a bar, shouts an order at the bartender, drinks loudly, coughs, spills his drink, drops the glass, and then walks out without paying. Another tippler asks the bartender, "What's wrong with him?" The bartender says, "Oh, he is a free radical!"

- **A deuterium walks into a bar**
  A deuterium walks into a bar and the bartender asks, "Seen any tritiums lately?". The deuterium answers, "Yeah but that lowlife was already in a state of decay."

- **A neutron and a neutrino walk into a bar**
  A neutron and a neutrino walk into a bar and order drinks. To the neutron, the bartender says, "For you, no charge!". To the neutrino, the bartender, "That will be two bucks." The neutrino is upset by this and says, "Hey, I am also neutral." For that, the bartender says, "Yeah, but he carries more weight."

- **What did Earth say to Moon?**
  "You seem to be hiding something behind your back."

- **What did Moon say to Earth?**
  "It's nothing. You always need to look at the bright side!"

Chemistry Jokes

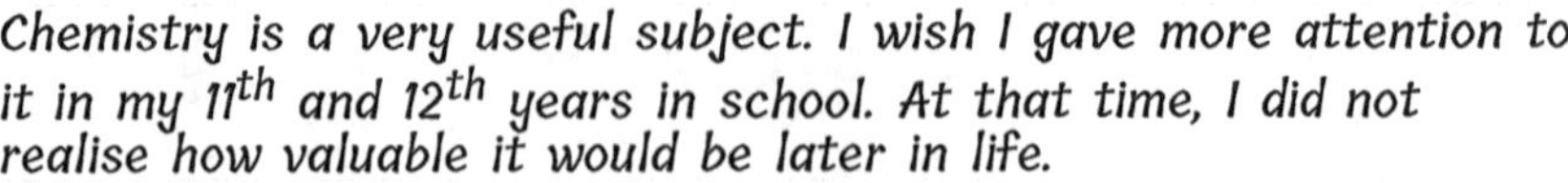

Chemistry is a very useful subject. I wish I gave more attention to it in my 11th and 12th years in school. At that time, I did not realise how valuable it would be later in life.

- **What did hydroiodic acid say?**
  It said 'HI'.

- **What did the hydrogen atom say about the helium atom?**
  "**He** sounds funny."

- **What did carbon say when it was accused of Climate Change?**
  "I **C**."

- **Enzyme**

  Fatty Acid 1: What do you think of that enzyme?
  Fatty Acid 2: I don't trust him. He is always starting something.

- **What happened to nitric acid after water decided to leave?**
  It left him fuming.

- **What did 0.81 mole of a substance say to 0.36 mole of the same?**
  "There is a mole among us."

- **What did Mrs. Mendeleev say?**
  She said Mr. Mendeleev was in his elements today.

- **Why was the ester acting so sweet?**
  It was under the influence of alcohol.

- **What did the alkali say to the metal?**
  "All your base are belong to us."

- **What did sodium say when asked to leave the oil business?**
  It said 'NaH'.

- **What did the acetic acid say?**
  It maintained an ascetic silence.

- **What did lye do to make water angry?**
  Lye developed a caustic attitude.

- **What did one hydrogen ion say to another?**
  "Between you and me, we are missing two neutrons."

- **What did the lithium ion say to his psychiatrist?**
  "Everyone takes lithium when they are depressed but what do we take when we are depressed?"

- **What did the psychiatrist say to the lithium ion?**
  "You are not like everyone. You need to take charge!"

- **What did the psychiatrist say to the beryllium atom?**
  "You can **Be** what you want to **Be**."

- *New Scientist* **Humour**
  The *New Scientist* magazine used to have a humour section. One item was about a letter from an American who had lived in India for several years. A sure-fire method he had developed to kill cockroaches was to use rice flour mixed with boric acid. (Boric acid powder is available in drug stores as an antimicrobial

agent.) What was so funny about it? The item was titled "cereal killer".

- **Inertness**

  > **Hydrogen ion**: Did the Neon atom speak to you?
  > **Oxygen ion**: Nah, I couldn't get a reaction.

- **Why did the magnesium roll refuse to talk to the CO2 cannister?**
  There was a lot of heat between them.

- **Did you know this about aluminium?**
  Metallic aluminium reacts with air to form aluminium oxide. This aluminium oxide forms a hard impermeable layer over the metal making it naturally resistant to corrosion.

- **What is the name for sand when it used in some processed foods to prevent clumping?**
  Silicon dioxide.

Industrially purified powdered sand.

- **Name the chemical used to remove the brown colour from cane sugar and make it sparkling white?**
  Bone char (burnt bones) – made up of mostly of phosphorous/calcium compounds and pure carbon.

Brown sugar or unrefined sugar does not go through this cleaning process. However, lack of demand has made it more expensive.

- **What did silicon say?**
  Si said "**Yes,** I am everywhere."

- **Name the chemical used in soft drinks in place of citric acid?**
  Phosphoric acid – more economical by weight.

Phosphoric acid is the main component of rust remover.

- **Which everyday-use substance is straight out of hell?**
  Vulcanized rubber – made in combination with fire and brimstone (sulphur).

- **What happens when sulphur becomes frustrated?**
  It gets selfurious.

- **What did chlorine gas say?**
  It felt heavy and would like to just 'hang around'.

- **Bleach and DDT**
  Most Tamilians have seen the Koundamani–Senthil movie நினைவு சின்னம் where Senthil sprays pesticide on sweets in Koundamani's store to kill flies. I saw something similar in a general store. Someone had paid for bleaching powder but was given a DDT packet instead. This happened when the owner left a boy in charge of the shop when he went to his home for lunch. To save printing costs, the packets were unmarked and looked the same. Fortunately, the customer realized the mix-up before the contents were dropped in the well. Both pesticides and bleach are manufactured, stored and sold without any standards and precautions in our country. These items should be clearly marked and stored in different places both at the store and at home.

- **What did argon gas say?**

"How **Ar** you?"

- **Cyanide**
The Sri Lankan Tamil terrorist group LTTE was famous for using cyanide vials for a quick-kill suicide poison. They were not the only ones. Many among Hitler's immediate circle used it to end their lives. So, did many British spies. KCN has also been a favourite among many scientists. Even the computer scientist, Alan Turing, used cyanide to exit this world. What maroons, as Bugs Bunny would say! Exposed to moist air, KCN powder emits hydrogen cyanide (HCN) gas, which is also poisonous. Exposed to water, it readily dissolves and leaks. The few minutes to reach unconsciousness may seem like an eternity. Death can sometimes take up to an hour. Exposure to an insufficient quantity can result in permanent organ damage and lifelong suffering. Accidental exposure is also a high possibility, particularly in a rough-and-tumble work environment such as terrorism or spying.

- **What did iron say its last wish was?**
It wanted to rust in peace.

- **What did copper sulfide say on the way to the smelter?**
"**C u** later."

- **What did arsenic say when it was found to be toxic?**
As you like it.

- **Where is calcium?**
It went to get a $CaBr_2$.

- **What got zirconium arrested?**
It was trying to pass of as a real diamond.

Many years back, zirconium was advertised as 'American diamonds' in newspapers.

- **Knock Knock**
  Who is there?
  Molly.
  Molly who?
  Molybdenum!

- **How does silver halide remember everything?**
It has a photographic memory.

- **What happened to silver-zinc batteries?**
That was a long time AgO ($Ag_2O \cdot Ag_2O_3$).

- **What did ruthenium say?**
"Who **R u**?"

- **Is indium coming to the party?**
Indium said it was **In**.

- **Knock Knock**
  Who is there?
  Aunty.
  Aunty who?
  Antimony!

- **Why did the iodine molecule break up?**

The atoms refused to see 'I' to 'I'.

- **What did cæsium say?**
  Nothing. It was too soft to say anything.

- **What did barium say?**
  "Who has the guts to take me?"

- **What did tungsten say rubidium?**
  "It's **W**."

- **What did iridium say to rubidium?**
  No idea. It was very very hard to get a reaction.

- **Does mercury like the new place?**
  Yes. It is adjusting to the pressure well.

- **How is lead finding the new place?**
  It could not stand the heat and felt like it was going to melt.

- **What did bismuth say to iron?**
  Nothing. Bismuth was repelled by it.

- **What did astatine say?**
  Don't know. That half-life is difficult to get **At**.

- **Knock Knock**
  > Who is there?
  > Ruth.
  > Ruth who?
  > Rutherfordium.

- **How do you hail uranium?**
  "Hey, U!"

- **Why did Mendelevium complain to the UN (United Nations)?**
  Because many countries were trying to isolate it.

- **What do ordinary metals say when they meet rare earth metals?**
  "Long time. No see."

- **What do you get when you mix an acid and alkyl ion and leave it for 24 hours?**
  Esterday.

- **What did the centrifuge say to the test tube?**
  "I can take you out for a spin."

- **Why did the soap refuse to go out with the salt?**
  It didn't want to precipitate something.

- **Why did the precipitate say?**
  It was tired of all the actions and reactions when what it wanted was just to settle down somewhere quiet.

- **Why did the catalyst say?**
  It was tired of all the actions and reactions when what it wanted was just to get back to how it was in the beginning.

- **Why did the catalyst say?**
  It was tired of the slow pace of everything and just wanted to speed things up a bit.

- **Why will crude oil never make it as a secret agent?**
  Because it cracks under pressure.

- **Why does 1 gram of any molecule always get upset with the chemist?**
  Because the chemist accuses it of being a mole.

- **What did one mole say to another?**
  "You dig me?"

- **How did one mole stop fighting with another?**
  They tried to find a solution.

- **What did one mole say to another on October 23?**
  "Happy Mole Day!"

- **Which synthetic fibre is this close to being in league with the Devil?**
  Nylon 6/6.

- **Which synthetic fibre is in league with the Devil?**
  Nylon 66/6.

- **What kind of music do lab technicians like to listen?**
  Instrumental music.

Biology Jokes

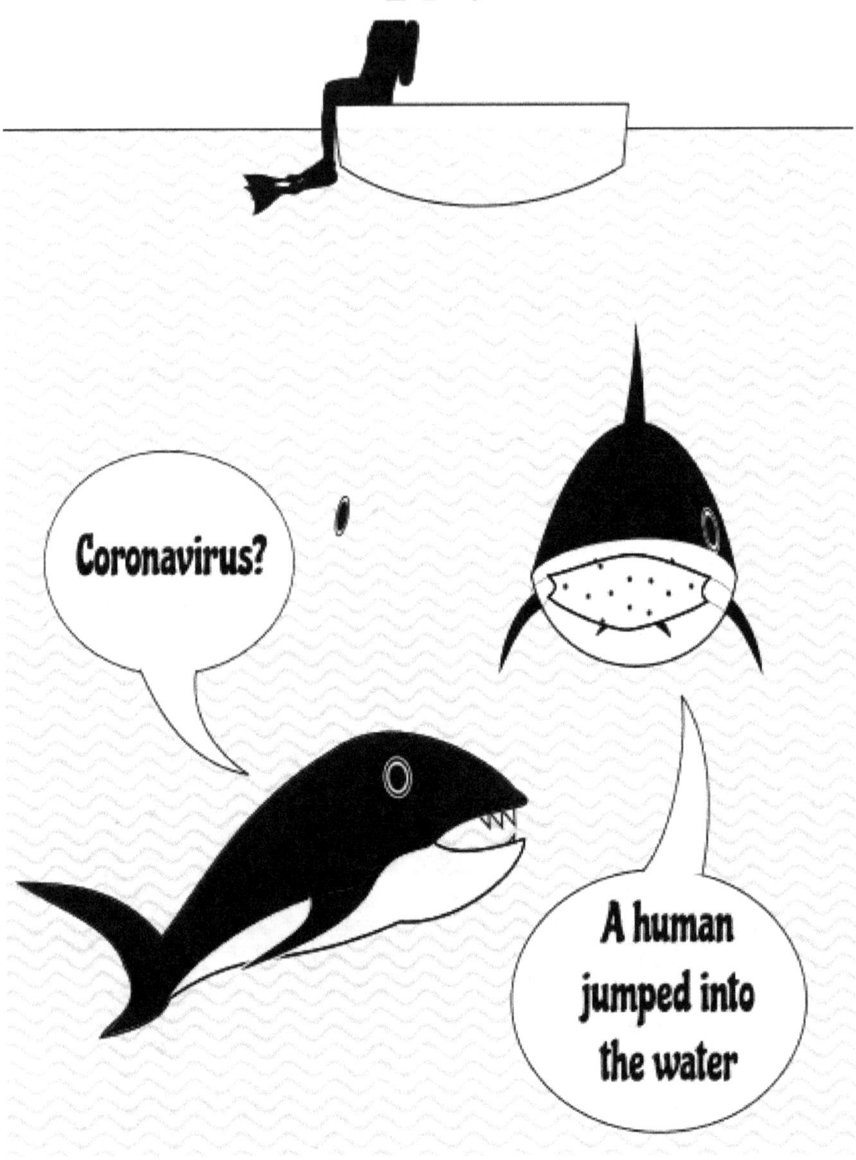

Biology was my favourite subject in school because it was the easiest to remember. Like with chemistry, this subject becomes very useful throughout your life.

- **Nutting like it**

Peanut: You know, we are both legumes.
Soybean: No, you are nuts!

- **If an astronomer was born as a fish, what kind would it be?**
  Telescopefish.

- **What happens when a tsetse fly bites a government official?**
  The official throws away his sleeping pills.

- **Name the happiest plant group.**
  Algae – They are all gay (happy).

Scientifically, algae are not plants. Algae are chlorophyll-producing plant-like living organisms that lack the traditional stomata, xylem and phloem cells. A good example is seaweed.

- **Why is xylem more believable than phloem?**
  Phloem can say anything but it does not hold water.

- **What country do you get when you cross an algae and a microbe?**
  Algeria.

- **Why was the fruticose angry with the toadstool?**
  The mushroom **lichen**ed it to an algae.

- **Name the vegetable that desperately needs to chill?**
  Hot potatoes.

- **What do banana trees like to read?**
  Yellow journalism.

- **What kind of computer games do touch-me-not plants hate to play?**

Stimulation.

- **If an politician was born as a fish, what kind would it be?**
  Megamouth shark.

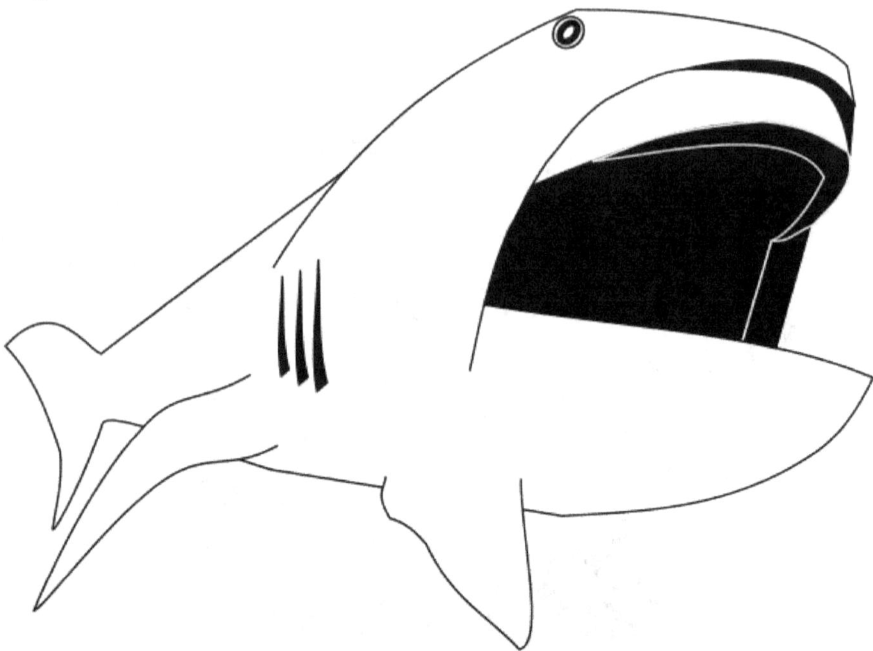

- **If a chicken was born as a fish, what kind would it be?**
  Roosterfish.

- **What would happen if a mollusc was made to ride an elevator?**
  It would clam up.

- **How did the elephant react when the ant asked him about his weight?**
  He became **lipid** with anger.

- **What does the elephant's yearbook say about him?**
  "Most likely to never forget a slight, not even from an ant."

If you want the backgrounder for this joke, read the section *Elephant And Ant Jokes* .

- **What does the water anole's yearbook say about him?**
  "Most likely to move around with an air about him."

This creature carries a bubble around its head to stay under water and breathe.

- **Why did the llama refuse to drink with the camel?**
  It was a Bactrian camel.

- **How does a rhizome step out of the kitchen?**
  Gingerly.

- **Why was the snail sent to the psychiatrist?**
  He appeared withdrawn.

- **What did the psychiatrist tell the snail?**

That to get back on his feet, he really needs to come out of his shell.

- **What did the WBC (White Blood Cell) tell the virus?**
  "Are you are sure you're really dead?"

- **Corona**

  Virus 1: Who is that walking with his nose up in the air?**
  Virus 2: He is nothing to be sneezed at. He caused a pandemic.

- **What did the DNA tell the transcriptase enzyme?**
  "Should we go through this all over again?"

- **What did the DNA tell the viral transcriptase enzyme?**
  "You've got everything in reverse."

- **Two X chromosomes walk into a bar?**
  Two X chromosomes walk into a bar and one of them says, "Let's sit next that fem." The other chromosome asks, "Y?"

- **What did one mutant say to another?**
  "I know I have a few faults but I think they are just aberrations."

- **What did the mushroom say to another?**
  "This is my last straw."

- **What did one silverfish say to another?**
  "This jokebook is just trash."

- **What kind of music do bats like to listen?**
  Acoustic.

- **What kind of music do sharks like to listen?**
  Jazz.

- **What kind of music do ants like to listen?**
  Acid Jazz.

Ants inject formic acid when they bite.

- **Which insect was named after a popular 60s music band?**
  Beetle.

- **Which 70s song do weevils like the most?**
  "We will... we will rock you" by Queen.

- **What kind of fiction do tadpoles like to read?**
  Young Adult.

- **What kind of music do frogs like to listen?**
  Adult contemporary.

- **How did the caterpillar couple make up?**
  He turned over a new leaf.

- **Why did the cicada couple break up?**
  She said he was a loudmouth.

- **Why did the dragonfly couple break up?**
  They refused to see eye-to-eye on many things.

- **How did the frog couple make up?**
  It required a leap of faith from both of them.

- **Why did the hermit crab couple break up?**

His shell was not big enough for the two of them.

- **Why did the hippopotamus couple break up?**
  He always left muddy footprints all over the floor.
- **Why did the jellyfish couple break up?**
  They just drifted apart.
- **Why did the mollusc couple break up?**
  He did not have a funny bone in his body.
- **Why did the mosquito couple break up?**
  He accused her of being a blood sucker.
- **Why did the neanderthal couple break up?**
  He failed to evolve into a better person.
- **Why did the neanderthal couple make up?**
  He was such a fine specimen.
- **Why did the oyster couple make up?**
  Behind that hard exterior, he had a heart of gold... of pearl rather.
- **Why did the praying mantis couple break up?**
  She didn't. He was.
- **Why did the praying mantis eat her husband?**
  She couldn't have enough of him so he lost more than just his head.
- **How did the praying mantis couple make up?**
  It was a once-in-a-lifetime opportunity for him.
- **Which insect has been accused of worshipping false gods?**
  Praying mantis.
- **Why did the sea sponge couple break up?**
  He did not like her salty remarks.
- **How did the sea urchin couple break up?**
  He said she was prickly all the time and she said he was mentally unhinged.
- **Why did the silverfish couple break up?**
  She took a leaf out of his book.
- **How did the snail couple break up?**
  - They decided it was time move on with their lives separately.
  - He was becoming more senile.
  - She said that, in his home, she was treated only as a slug while in France she was considered quite a delicacy.
- **What does the shark's yearbook say about him?**
  "Most likely to put the bite on and not let go."
- **What does the starfish's yearbook say about him?**
  "Most likely to be a star in his own right."
- **Why did the toad couple make up?**
  - She still likes him, warts and all.
  - He was one toady reptile.
- **The Dragonfly**
  Dragonflies are interesting creatures. Check out information on dragonflies in your library. It is fascinating. Dragonflies fly fast, have great eyesight and

possess spectacular body strength relative to weight. Their flight trajectory is impossible to predict and their agility is impossible to match. A dragonfly has two big powerful eyes. They are so big that they seem to form the bulk of its head. The eyes are designed to track small insects while in flight.

- **What did the llama say to another?**
  "What's with the aloof expression?"

Medical Jokes

This section is for medical professionals.

- **Which superhero should only be examined with lead plates?**
  Superman – he has x-ray vision.

- **Which superhero is most likely to die from cancer?**
  Spiderman – he has radioactive blood.

- **Which superhero most likely needs a rabies shot?**
  Batman.

- **What would happen if medicines had a better love-life?**
  The pills would not be so bitter.

- **Why did the polar bear couple break up?**
  Bipolar disorder.

- **Why are lift operators never depressed?**
  They listen to elevator music all the time.

- **How did the ghost couple break up?**
  They were mortified when it happened.

- **What do morticians like to read?**
  Obituaries.

- **What did one corpse say to another?**
  "What's with the deadpan expression?"

- **Biting Humour**

    Canine teeth: What has two or three legs but doesn't go anywhere?
    Incisor teeth: What?
    Canine teeth: Molars.

- **An incisive 'Gift For Someone You Love' jingle**

    Premolar 1: I am too small for candy...
    Premolar 2: I am too big for biscuits...
    Molar 1: But I think you are just right for Amul Chocolate.

- **What did one incisor say to another?**
  "We are surrounded by sharp characters."

- **What do dentists call molar tooth?**
  "Money makers."

- **What do dentists call an infected root canal?**
  "The real deal."

- **How did the dentist die?**
  He told the vampire, "You have a serious overbite problem. Please look in this mirror."

- **What kind of music do surgeons like to listen?**
  Opera.

- **What kind of music do anæsthetists like to listen?**
  Trance.

- **How does a surgeon feel after a good night's sleep?**
  A sharp operator.

- **What kind of films do ER physicians like to see?**
  Troma Movies.

- **Why did the doctor couple break up?**
  - She was sick of his attitude.
  - A cure for her madness has not been invented yet.
  - She was testing his patience.
  - She was taxing his patience.
  - Their intense hatred for each other was quite palpable.
  - When it came to housework, he was Dr. Dolittle.
  - She said she did not need a second-opinion.
  - She gave him a taste of his own medicine and he did not like it.

- **Why did the doctor couple make up?**
  - They decided to give it another shot.
  - What cannot be cured has to be endured.
  - He bore her no ill feeling.

- **Why did the dentist couple break up?**
  - Frequent fights with her left him toothless.
  - She drilled into him that any resistance was futile.

- **Why did the dentist couple make up?**
  Dental insurance is cheaper under the family plan.

- **Why did the acupuncturist couple break up?**
  She easily punctured his ego.

- **Why did the radiologist couple break up?**
When a radiologist says that her husband has absolutely nothing in his head...

- **Acupuncturist**

    Doctor 1: Did you attend the funeral of the acupuncturist?
    Doctor 2: I did. The eulogies indicate that he was quite a prick.

- **Anæsthesiologist**

    Doctor 1: Did you attend the funeral of the anæsthesiologist?
    Doctor 2: I did. Many of the mourners did not feel he was really gone.

- **Cardiologist**

    Doctor 1: Did you attend the funeral of the cardiologist?
    Doctor 2: I did. He seems to have touched many hearts.

- **Chiropractor**

    Doctor 1: Did you attend the funeral of the chiropractor?
    Doctor 2: I did. The eulogies were quite moving.

- **Dentist**

    Doctor 1: Did you attend the funeral of the dentist?
    Doctor 2: I did. Many of the mourners had indeed given their back teeth to him.

- **Dermatologist**

    Doctor 1: Did you attend the funeral of the dermatologist?
    Doctor 2: I did. Time will be a salve for those who had known him.

- **Endocrinologist**

    Doctor 1: Did you attend the funeral of the endocrinologist?
    Doctor 2: I did. His widow was inconsolable. You could hear **her moan** and cry all the time.

- **Gastroenterologist**

    Doctor 1: Did you attend the funeral of the gastroenterologist?
    Doctor 2: I did. Some mourners vented their bile at Fate for taking him away.

- **Gynæcologist**

    Doctor 1: Did you attend the funeral of the gynæcologist?
    Doctor 2: I did. Mourners came from yEast and Evista.

- **Hæmatologist**

    Doctor 1: Did you attend the funeral of the hæmatologist?
    Doctor 2: I did. There were **Few** who did not miss him.

- **Immunologist**

    Doctor 1: Did you attend the funeral of the immunologist?
    Doctor 2: I did. Emotions ran wild through the congregation.

- **Neurologist**

    Doctor 1: Did you attend the funeral of the neurologist?
    Doctor 2: I did. Everyone tried to steady their nerves.

- **Ophthalmologist**

    Doctor 1: Did you attend the funeral of the ophthalmologist?

Doctor 2: I did. There wasn't a dry eye.

- **Pædiatrist**

  Doctor 1: Did you attend the funeral of the pædiatrist?
  Doctor 2: I did. All mourners were given free candy.

- **Pulmonologist**

  Doctor 1: Did you attend the funeral of the pulmonologist?
  Doctor 2: I did. The air was filled with sadness.

- **Psychiatrist**

  Doctor 1: Did you attend the funeral of the psychiatrist?
  Doctor 2: I did. The eulogies were couched in confessions.

- **Radiologist**

  Doctor 1: Did you attend the funeral of the radiologist?
  Doctor 2: I did. Most mourners said he saw through their failings.

- **Speech therapist**

  Doctor 1: Did you attend the funeral of the speech therapist?
  Doctor 2: I did. Some mourners were still lost for words.

- **Urologist**

  Doctor 1: Did you attend the funeral of the urologist?
  Doctor 2: I did. People wondered if his death could have been a **void**ed.

- **Acupuncturist referral**

  Doctor: Why was the patient referred to the acupuncturist?
  Nurse: His wife said he had absolutely no feelings.

- **Anæsthesiologist referral**

  Doctor: Why was the anæsthesiologist called *during* surgery?
  Surgeon: Somebody was reading the bill and the patient came to his senses.

- **Cardiologist referral**

  Doctor: Why was the patient referred to the cardiologist?
  Nurse: To see if he can take the shock of the bill.

- **Why did the headless chicken cross the road?**
  If it was anything, it was all heart!

- **Dermatologist referral**

  Doctor: Why was the patient referred to the dermatologist?
  Nurse: The sight of the bill made his skin itch uncontrollably.

- **Dentist referral**

  Doctor: Why was the patient referred to the dentist?
  Nurse: The growing number of bills left his teeth shattered.

- **Gastroenterologist referral**

  Doctor: Why was the patient referred to the gastroenterologist?
  Nurse: He couldn't take it anymore.

- **Hæmatologist referral**

  Doctor: Why was the patient referred to the hæmatologist?
  Nurse: He claimed he had an iron constitution.

- **Immunologist referral**

  > **Doctor**: Why was the patient referred to the immunologist?
  > **Nurse**: She had an infectious smile.

- **Ophthalmologist referral**

  > **Doctor**: Why was the patient referred to the ophthalmologist?
  > **Nurse**: He said he was seeing too many digits in the bill.

- **Obstetrician referral**

  > **Doctor**: Why was this diabetic referred to the obstetrician?
  > **Nurse**: He said he was demanding sweets only because of his inner child.

- **Pædiatrist referral**

  > **Doctor**: Why was this adult diabetic referred to the pædiatrist?
  > **Nurse**: We didn't. The patient went there to get the free candy.

- **Psychiatrist referral**

  > **Doctor**: Why was the patient referred to the psychiatrist?
  > **Nurse**: He said the growing number of bills was driving him crazy.

- **Radiologist referral**

  > **Doctor**: Why was the comedian referred to the radiologist?
  > **Nurse**: He said something was wrong with his funny bone.

- **Speech therapist referral**

  > **Doctor**: Why was the patient referred to the Speech therapist?
  > **Nurse**: He became speechless when he was told about all the tests and procedures he had to take before his physician could recommend a treatment.

- **What do proctologists like to read?** Just the colophon.

- **A nervous reaction**

  > **Doctor 1**: Why did the patient kick that doctor?
  > **Doctor 2**: The neurologist struck a raw nerve.

- **The strongest muscle**

  > **Doctor 1**: Did he really burst his aorta?
  > **Doctor 2**: No. That diagnosis was made in a lighter vein.

Pun Jokes

Did you look square in the eye?

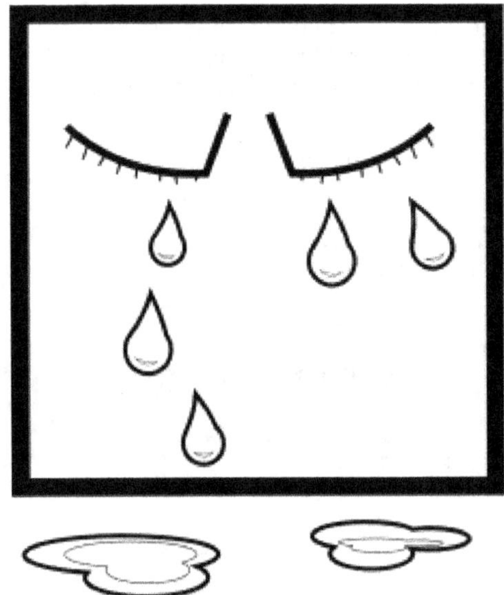

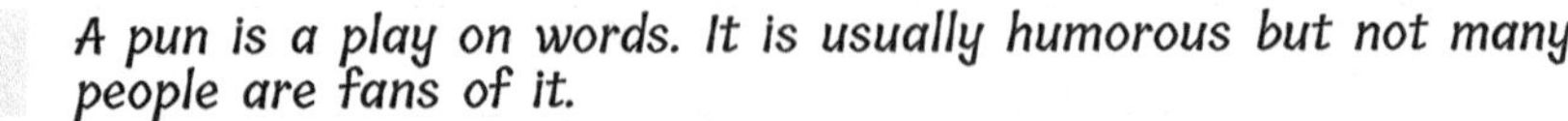

A pun is a play on words. It is usually humorous but not many people are fans of it.

- **What kind of chicken do contortionists like to order?**
  Boneless Chicken.
- **What kind of chicken do efficiency experts like to order?**

Butter Chicken.

- **What kind of chicken do psychopaths like to order?**
  Scaredy Chicken.

- **What kind of chicken do zombies like to order?**
  Headless Chicken.

- **What kind of chicken do bored people like to order?**
  Chicken Bordelaise.

- **What kind of chicken do government contractors like to order?**
  Tendoori Chicken.

- **What kind of chicken do government employees like to order?**
  Roost Chicken.

- **What kind of chicken do South-East Asians like to order?**
  Malay Chicken.

- **What kind of chicken do South Americans like to order?**
  Chile Chicken.

- **Why did the archeologist cross the road?**
  He had a bone to pick.

- **Why did the skeleton cross the road?**
  To stop the archeologist.

- **Why did the dog cross the road?**
  This was a bone of contention.

- **Why did the psychopath cross the road?**
  He wanted to give them a piece of his mind.

- **Why did the Asian guy cross the road?**
  To pick up some Chinese.

- **What did Japanese soldiers eat when they occupied Singapore?**
  They ordered Chinese.

This joke has a very serious historical meaning.

- **Winner takes it all**
  A man went to a restaurant and ordered lobster. When the plate was placed before him, the lobster was in numerous pieces. The man asked the waiter, "Why is my lobster so broken up?" The waiter answered, "The creatures fight inside the tank and they break off each other's limbs." The man then said, "Okay, bring me the winner." The waiter agreed and came back after a few minutes. When the new plate was placed before him, the man noticed that the new lobster was mostly intact but still had two parts missing. He said, "This one does not have a claw and something else too." The waiter said "Sir, this is indeed the victor but victory cost him an arm and a leg."

In an early edition of this book, I credited the first half of this joke to *Reader's Digest*. Later, I found it in an episode of *Abbott and Costello Show* . The second half of the joke is my invention.

- **What did one nostalgia say to another?**
  "You are not what you used to be."

- **What did one Indian lemon say to another?**
  "We are in a real pickle."

- **What did one American cucumber say to another?**
  Same as the Indian lemon.

- **What did one table leg say to another?**
  "You scared? Why are you shaking?"

- **What did the blade say to the windmill?**
  "I am a big fan of yours."

- **What did one antelope say to another?**
  "You gotta buck?"

- **What did the crow say to the scarecrow?**
  "You are fooling nobody so don't crow about it!"

- **What did the scarecrow say to the crow?**
  "But, my hands are tied!"

- **What did the string instrument say to the flute?**
  "You sound hollow."

- **What did the flute say to the string instrument?**
  "Please don't harp on it."

- **What did one typewriter say to another?**
  "I am trying to make a good impression."

- **What does the beautician's yearbook say about him?**
  "Most likely to make your hair curl."

- **What does the chicken plucker's yearbook say about him?**
  "Most likely to rustle up some serious feathers."

- **What does the clown's yearbook say about him?**
  "Most likely to be surrounded by buffoons."

- **What does the humorist's yearbook say about him?**
  "Most likely to try to humour himself than others."

- **What does the jester's yearbook say about him?**
  "Most unlikely to run away from a pun."

- **What does the joke writer's yearbook say about him?**
  "Most likely to laugh at his own jokes."

- **What does the wit's yearbook say about him?**
  "Most likely to wit than have wisdom."

- **What does the psychopath's yearbook say about him?**
  "Most likely to leave a serious impact on people."

- **What does the sumo wrestler's yearbook say about him?**
  "Most likely to head a large corporation."

- **What does the usher's yearbook say about him?**
  "Most likely to open a door and shine a path for others."

- **What does the vagrant's yearbook say about him?**
  "Most likely to see the world."

- **What does the vandal's yearbook say about him?**
  - "Most likely to paint the town red."
  - "Most likely to make his mark on the world."

- **What did the exercise book say?**
  "I have many problems."

- **What did the key say to the exercise book?**
  "I've got answers to all your problems."

- **What did the non-detailed book say?**
  "I do not need you to explain everything."

- **What did the answer sheet say to the question paper?**
  "Is it about those problems? I can explain everything."

- **What did the priest say when he asked the parents sign the exorcism waiver?**
  "The devil is in the detail."

- **What did the policeman write in his report after he caught a ghost speeding?**
  "He was in really high spirits."

- **What did the policeman write in his report after he caught the screaming banshee speeding?**
  "She was in a tearing hurry."

- **What musical instrument eats healthy, does regular exercise and gets enough sleep?**
  The fiddle. That's why everyone says 'fit as a fiddle'.

- **What happened when the ghost tripped over a bucket?**
  It turned *pail*.

- **Why did the quadrilateral fight with the circle?**
  The circle looked square in the eye.

- **Why did zero go to the psychiatrist?**
  Everyone said he would amount to nothing.

- **Why was the alien looking at the remote instead of the television?**
  He was doing remote viewing.

- **How do you transport an elephant in a train?**
  You give it a wide berth.

- **What do Egyptian mummies like to read?**
  Some rag.

- **What do zombies like to read?**
  Some dirty rag.

- **What do government employees like to read?**
  Deductive fiction.

- **What do guns like to read?**
  Magazines.

- **What do hair dressers hate to see on TV?**
Election coverage.

- **What do Italians like to read?**
Romantic fiction.

- **What happens when plants read yellow journalism?**
They go bananas.

- **What do politicians like to read?**
Grime fiction.

- **What do psychiatrists like to read?**
Entertainment news.

- **What do pyromaniacs like to see on TV?**
Burning Issue.

Indian English-language TV news channel viewers will know what this is.

- **What do spies like to read?**
The classifieds.

- **What do vandals like to see on TV?**
Breaking news.

- **Why did the nun cross the road?**
None of your business.

- **Why did the lightning cross the road?**
Someone stole its thunder.

- **Why did the Devil cross the road?**
Speak of the Devil...

- **What did one clown say to another?**
"What's with the silly expression?"

- **What did one clock say to another?**
"What's with the alarmed expression?"

- **What did one crossword say to another?**
"What's with the puzzled expression?"

- **What did one remote say to another?**
"What's with the muted expression?"

- **What did one gargoyle say to another?**
"What's with the dour expression?"

- **What did one statue say to another?**
"What's with the chiselled expression?"

- **What did one washing machine say to another?**
"What's with the agitated expression?"

- **What happened when the doughnut rolled away and fell to the floor?**
It was roundly criticized.

- **Why did the police state persecute the toad?**
For thought crimes.

- **How do you transport a hippopotamus in a train?**
Using a hypocrate.

- **Why was the dragon so happy?**
  It was fired up and ready to go.

- **Why was the human cannonball so happy?**
  It was fired and ready to go home.

- **What do traffic lights learn in school?**
  Sign language.

- **What do statues do in school?**
  Studied silence.

- **What do mannequins learn in school?**
  A pose-itive attitude.

- **Do mannequins talk?**
  No, but their body language do tell a whole story.

- **What did one vampire say to another?**
  "Can I drop in for a bite?"

- **Which magazine should you trust more – *Outlook* or *Outlook Money*?**
  Outlook because *Money* talks.

- ***Time* challenges *Newsweek* to a race. Which magazine will win?**
  Time. Because time flies.

- ***Time* magazine challenges Superman to a race. Who will win?**
  Time. Because time [and tide] waits for none while Superman will stop for a cat that is stuck on a tree.

- ***Time* versus *Life*. Which magazine is the most original?**
  Time. Because life imitates art.

- ***Time* versus *Life*. Which magazine will be your friend when you are in the wrong?**
  Life. Because time will tell.

- ***Time* versus *Life*. Which magazine will be useful in a medical emergency?**
  Time. Because time is a great healer.

- ***Time* versus *Life*. Which magazine is better in other kinds of emergencies?**
  Life. Because desperate times calls for desperate measures.

- ***Time* versus *Life*. Which magazine is a better basketball player?**
  Time. Because life is short.

- ***Time* versus *Life*. Which magazine is worth more?**
  Life. Because time is money.

- ***Time* versus *Life*. Which magazine will last the longest?**
  Time. Because life begins at 40.

- **What happens when you give alcohol to a chicken?**
  Chicken rolls.

- **Why did the goat cross the road?**
  Don't know. It refused to be quoted.

- **Why should you not look a gift horse in the mouth?**
  You might encounter some horsetility.

The word 'horsetility' is from an old joke book.

- **What do you get when you teach judo to a pig?**
  Pork chops.

- **What did one nailgun say to another?**
  "I am going to try another tack."

- **What did one sheet of paper say to another?**
  "What's with the blank expression?"

- **Tautology**

    Tautology 1: Do I have to repeat myself?
    Tautology 2: You can say that again.

- **What would happen if an amusement park was named after a girl named Anna?**
  It is anathema.

- **What would happen if a vampire bites a government official?**
  The vampire stops sleeping in a coffin and starts sleeping on a desk.

- **What would happen if a vampire bites Spiderman?**
  The vampire gets cancer because Spiderman has radioactive blood.

- **What would happen if a zombie gets a registered letter?**
  The tax department has been informed of his/her return.

- **What does it mean when a vampire gets bitten by a zombie?**
  The vampire starts working for the tax department.

- **What would happen if you bother a butcher when he is in the freezer?**
  He might give you a cold shoulder.

- **What would happen if someone writes a biography of a judge?**
  You could *cover* the *judge* with a *book.*

- **What would happen if fate had sticky tape?**
  It would seal itself.

- **What would happen if night was exhausted?**
  It would call it a day.

- **What kind of music do Communists like to listen?**
  Classical.

- **What kind of music do Socialists like to listen?**
  Underground.

- **What kind of music do Fascists like to listen?**
  Corporate.

- **What kind of music do death row inmates hate to listen?**
  Chamber.

- **What kind of music do escaped jail inmates like to listen?**
  Indie.

- **What kind of music do stamp collectors like to listen?**
  Country.

- **What kind of music do balloons hate?**
  Pop.

- **What kind of music do spelling-bee contestants like to listen?**
  Gospel.

- **What kind of music do psychopaths like to listen?**
  Psychedelic.
- **What kind of music do serial killers like to listen?**
  Progressive.
- **What kind of music do ham-radio operators like to listen?**
  New wave.
- **What kind of music do zombies like to listen?**
  Background.
- **What kind of music do vampires like to listen?**
  Contemporary.
- **What kind of music do people chased by vampires like to listen?**
  Religious.
- **What kind of music do ghosts like to listen?**
  Spiritual.
- **What kind of music do bomb-making terrorists hate to listen?**
  Metal.
- **What kind of music do condemned prisoners in France hate to listen?**
  Death metal.
- **What happened when Louis XVI came home late?**
  Marie Antoinette just lost her head.
- **What kind of music do interred zombies hate to listen?**
  Heavy metal.
- **What kind of music do tight-rope walkers hate to listen?**
  Dance.
- **What kind of music do performing musicians hate to listen?**
  Mobile phone ring tones.
- **What kind of music do kids hate to listen after they get into trouble?**
  Folk.
- **What kind of music do all the animals and people in the section *Cross The Road Jokes* like to listen?**
  Crossover.
- **What kind of music do electrocuted people like to listen?**
  Fusion.
- **What kind of fiction do mediums like to read?**
  Seance fiction.
- **What kind of movies do dry cleaners like to see?**
  Costume drama.
- **What computer games do attorneys like to play?**
  Rule-playing (RPG)
- **What computer game do acupuncturists like to play?**
  Pins of Persia.
- **What computer games do professional hitmen like to play?**
  First-Person Shooter (FPS).
- **What computer game do psychopaths like to play?**

Max Payne.

- **What computer game do junk callers like to play?**
  Halo.
- **What computer game do ghosts like to play?**
  Mortal Kombat.
- **What kind of films do vampires like to go to see?**
  Historical drama.
- **What kind of films do zombies like to go to see?**
  Reanimated.
- **What happens when a terrorist becomes nostalgic?**
  It begins with a blast from the past.
- **What happens when a moray eel goes to a saloon?**
  The barber faces a moral dilemma.
- **What kind of haircut does a pilot get when he wants to motivate his team?**
  A crew cut.
- **What kind of haircut does an accountant get when work piles up?**
  A summer cut.
- **What kind of haircut does a drummer get when he goes to the saloon?**
  Bangs.
- **What kind of haircut does a terrorist get when bites the grenade and throws the pin?**
  Blowout.
- **What kind of haircut does a juvenile get when parents bug him?**
  Bee hive.
- **What kind of haircut does a lynx get when he goes to the saloon?**
  Bob cut.
- **What kind of haircut does a cricketer get when he goes to the saloon?**
  Bowl cut.
- **What kind of haircut does a ram like to sport?**
  Double buns.
- **What kind of haircut do comb manufacturers are afraid of?**
  Dreadlocks.
- **What kind of haircut does an electrician get when he blows a fuse?**
  Spiked.
- **What did the lift say to the new operator?**
  "I can take you to high places."
- **What did one escalator say to another?**
  "There he goes again."
- **Why was the alphabet soup crying?**
  Some letters seemed to be missing.
- **What did the mulligatawny soup say?**
  "Am I hot or what?"
- **What did the turkey say?**
  "Friends, I am stuffed."

- **What did the beef say?**
  "Hey, I am on a roll."
- **What did the chicken say?**
  "I am in a real soup."
- **What did the duck say?**
  "I am dressed for dinner."
- **What did the fish say?**
  "Sorry, I am smoking."
- **What did the crab say?**
  "Don't strangle yourself. I am here to help."
- **What did the mutton say?**
  "I am feeling chopped up, already."
- **What did the noodle say?**
  "Folks, I want you to stay strong."
- **What did the lobster say?**
  "Yeah, let's hold hands."
- **What did the salad say?**
  "He is right. We are all in this together."
- **What did the onion rings say?**
  "You guys make me cry!"
- **What did the boiled egg say?**
  "I know I need to come out of my shell."
- **What did the raw egg say?**
  "Can I make a toast?"
- **What did the slice of bread say?**
  "I am toast!"
- **What did the wine say?**
  "I raise my glass to that."
- **What did the chef say?**
  "Stop it! You are making the guests nervous."
- **What did the restaurant review say?**
  "Chef Ram says his dishes really come to life and speak for themselves!"

Useful French Phrases

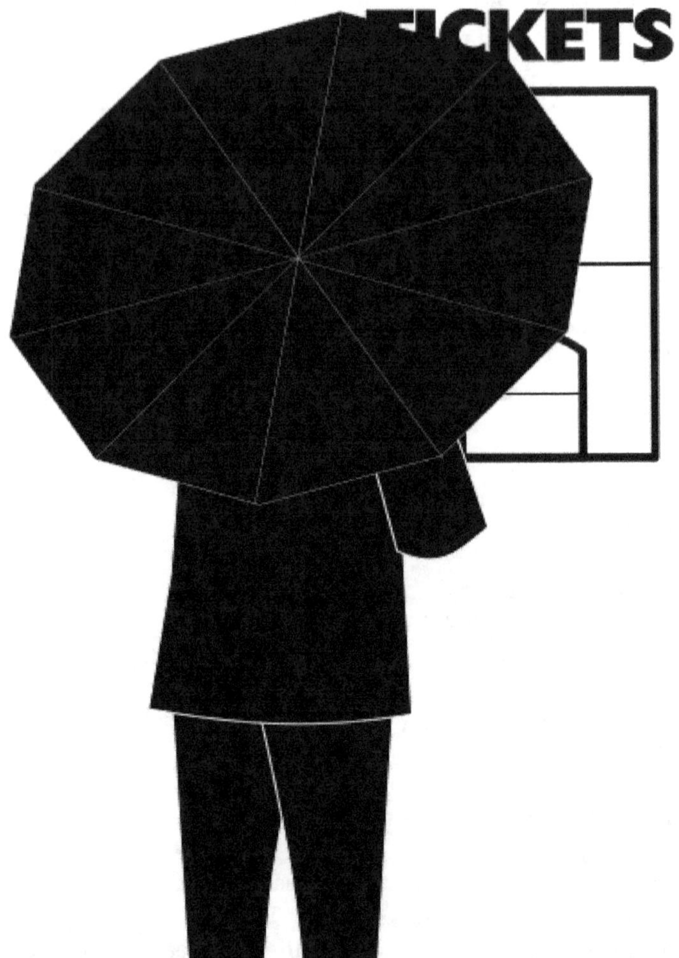

"One laissez-faire ticket and vive le difference. May the Lord have merci on you."

Lest this book be accused of misleading kids, the real meanings are provided sur place.

- **How do you say 'alternating current (AC)' in French?**
  Au courant. [*well-informed*]

- **How do you say 'the ape ate the bun' in French?**
Bon apetit. [*good appetite*]

- **How do you say 'we want a bun' in French?**
Bon vivant. [*well-to-do person*]

- **How do you say 'ticket price' in French?**
Chargé d'affaires. [*diplomat or person in-charge*]

- **How do you say 'The chef is hungry' in French?**
Chef d'œuvre. [*masterpiece*]

- **How do you say 'Check out the see-saw' in French?**
Comme ci, comme ça.

- **How do you say 'The commie is at fault' in French?**
Comme il faut. [*appropriately*]

- **How do you say 'know for sure' in French?**
Connoisseur. [*person with expert knowledge or taste*]

- **How do you say 'father's cup' in French?**
Coup de foudre. [*love at first sight*]

- **How do you say 'Grace's cup' in French?**
Coup de grâce. [*stroke of grace*]

- **How do you say 'look at your buns' in French?**
Cui bono. [*whose benefit*]

- **How do you say 'incurable disease' in French?**
Encore. [*repeat performance*]

- **How do you say 'angry elephant' in French?**
Enfant terrible. [*bad kid*]

- **How do you say 'we want to enter' in French?**
Enterré vivant. [*buried alive*]

- **How do you say 'ghost' in French?**
Esprit de corps. [*team spirit*]

- **How do you say 'we want to eat' in French?**
Être vivant. [*be alive*]

- **How do you say 'dead woman' in French?**
Femme fatale. [*attractive but dangerous woman*]

- **How do you say 'It's the cat's fault' in French?**
Faute de mieux. [*for a better*]

- **How do you say 'fat accomplice' in French?**
Fait accompli. [*irreversible fact*]

- **How do you say 'fake ID' in French?**
Faux pas. [*boo-boo*]

- **How do you say 'big pricks' in French?**
Grand prix. [*grand prize*]

- **How do you say "good-looking knife" in French?**
Haute couture. [*high fashion*]

- **How do you say 'hot quiz' in French?**
Haute cuisine. [*high-class cooking*]

- **How do you say 'devoured by a hungry horse' in French?**
  Hors d'œuvres.

- **How do you say 'unruly horse' in French?**
  Hors de combat. [*unfit for battle*]

- **How do you say 'in the way of the dodo' in French?**
  In toto. [*as a whole*]

- **How do you say 'low-priced ticket' in French?**
  Laissez-faire. [*free-for-all*]

- **How do you say 'mow the lawn' in French?**
  Mardi gras. [*Shrove Tuesday carnival*]

- **How do you say 'we want more' in French?**
  Mort vivant. [*animated corpse*]

- **How do you say 'never poor' in French?**
  Nouveau pauvre. [*newly poor*]

- **How do you say 'never rich' in French?**
  Nouveau riche. [*newly rich*]

- **How do you say 'objectionable artwork' in French?**
  Objet d'art. [*work of art*]

- **How do you say 'we want non-vegetarian food' in French?**
  Organisme vivant. [*living being*]

- **How do you say 'pour me a drink' in French?**
  Pardon moi. [*excuse me*]

- **How do you say 'something is blocking' in French?**
  Pièce de résistance. [*the best part*]

- **How do you say 'queue at the back' in French?**
  Quelle horreur.[*Oh, the horror!*]

- **How do you say 'run this way' in French?**
  Rendezvous. [*meeting*]

- **How do you say 'get up at three' in French?**
  Raison d'être. [*reason for existence*]

- **How do you say 'fear of misers' in French?**
  Savoir faire. [*act appropriately in all situations*]

- **How do you say 'is this your plate' in French?**
  S'il vous plaît. [*if you please*]

- **How do you say 'get us a table' in French?**
  Tableau vivant. [*body painting*]

- **How do you say 'give me the change' in French?**
  Vive la différence. [*celebrate the difference*]

Useful Latin Phrases

Lest this book be accused of misleading kids, the real meanings are provided in situ.

- **How do you say 'polygraph test' in Latin?**
  Alea iacta est. [*die is cast*]

- **How do you say 'cure for runny nose' in Latin?**
  Amicus curiae. [*friend of court*]

- **How do you say 'your fat friend' in Latin?**
  Amor fati. [*love of fate*]

- **How do you say 'Anna is as horrible as Bill is' in Latin?**
  Annus horribilis. [*horrible year*]

- **How do you say 'Anna is as miserable as Bill is' in Latin?**
  Annus mirabilis. [*miserable year*]

- **How do you say 'Anna is as terrible as Bill is' in Latin?**
  Annus terribilis. [*terrible year*]

- **How do you say 'Your aunty is a bum' in Latin?**
  Ante cibum. [*before meals*]

- **How do you say 'Your aunty is very dumb' in Latin?**
  Ante mortem. [*before death*]

- **How do you say 'the purée is watery' in Latin?**
  Aqua pura. [*pure water*]

- **How do you say 'Aurora is as much a bore as Al is' in Latin?**
  Aurora borealis. [*northern dawn*]

- **How do you say 'born fighter' in Latin?**
  Bona fides. [*good faith*]

- **How do you say 'bloating' in Latin?**
  Casus belli. [*causative event*]

- **How do you say 'as you were late, visa was not issued' in Latin?**
  Causa latet, vis est notissima. [*cause is not known while outcome is*]

- **How do you say 'empty cave' in Latin?**
  Caveat emptor. [*buyer beware*]

- **How do you say 'circling the house' in Latin?**
  Circulus vitiosus. [*vicious circle*]

- **How do you say 'I don't need more buns' in Latin?**
  Contra bonos mores. [*against good morals*]

- **How do you say 'there is no cure like liquor' in Latin?**
  Cor ad cor loquitur. [*heart speaks to heart*]

- **How do you say 'delicate zombie' in Latin?**
  Corpus delicti. [*offended body*]

- **How do you say 'angry zombie' in Latin?**
  Corpus vile. [*worthless body*]

- **How do you say 'the zombie are respectful' in Latin?**
  Corpus Juris Civilis. [*civil law*]

- **How do you say 'optimism corrupted by pessimism' in Latin?**
  Corruptio optimi pessima. [*the corruption of the best is the worst*]

- **How do you say 'sweet bun' in Latin?**
  Cui bono. [*for whose good*]

- **How do you say 'the fatso' in Latin?**
  De facto. [*in practice*]

- **How do you say 'this fatso' in Latin?**
  Ipso facto. [*after the fact*]

- **How do you say 'Hey, what's your bus number?' in Latin?**
  E pluribus unum. [*one among many*]

- **How do you say 'car with a wireless phone' in Latin?**
  Fons vitae caritas. [*love is the fountain of life*]

- **How do you say 'happy zombie' in Latin?**
  Habeas corpus. [*that you have the body*]

- **How do you say 'head East' in Latin?**
  Id est (i.e.) [*that is*]

- **How do you say 'a delicate fragrance?' in Latin?**
  In flagrante delicto. [*caught in the act of committing a crime*]

- **How do you say 'division and subtraction' in Latin?**
  Indivisibiliter ac inseparabiliter. [*indivisible and inseparable*]

- **How do you say 'his/her foolish parents?' in Latin?**
  In loco parentis. [*in place of parent*]

- **How do you say 'Look, he is standing' in Latin?**
  Locus standi. [*stands with the law*]

- **How do you say 'males are prohibited' in Latin?**
  Malum prohibitum. [*wrong because it is prohibited*]

- **How do you say 'my cup' in Latin?**
  Mea culpa. [*my fault*]

- **How do you say 'the mutants are mutating' in Latin?**
  Mutatis mutandis. [*after changing what needs to be changed*]

- **How do you say 'none sees how dumb it is' in Latin?**
  Nunc dimittis. [*Now you dismiss*]

- **How do you say 'Perpetually attached to the phone.' in Latin?**
  Perpetuum mobile. [*perpetual motion*]

- **How do you say 'I see no money [*on the table*].' in Latin?**
  Quid nunc. [*what now*]

- **How do you say 'got a buck or two' in Latin?**
  Quid pro quo. [*something in return of*]

- **How do you say 'the kid is going crazy' in Latin?**
  Quod erat demonstrandum. [*What was to be demonstrated*]

- **How do you say 'absurdly low prices' in Latin?**
  Reductio ad absurdum. [*ridiculous conclusion*]

- **How do you say 'quit staring' in Latin?**
  Stare decisis. [*recognizing previous decisions*]

- **How do you say 'Judy's submarine' in Latin?**
  Sub judice. [*currently under examination by a court*]

- **How do you say 'we roast possums' in Latin?**
  Vero possumus. [*yes, we can*]

Other Useful Foreign Phrases

"Adiós! Hasta la vista!"

The disclaimer from the previous chapter applies to this one too.

- **How do you say 'Get here and see the comet in the sky' in Danish?**
  Jeg er kommet til skade. [*I'm hurt*]

- **How do you say 'Hans is killing her' in Danish?**
  Hans kyllinger. [*his chickens*]

- **How do you say 'They raided him' in Danish?**
  De rådede ham. [*they advised him*]

- **How do you say 'Are you stupid' in Dutch?**
  Alstublieft. [*please*]

- **How do you say 'Who got hit' in Dutch?**
  Hoe gaat het. [*how are you*]

- **How do you say 'Who hit you' in Dutch?**
  Hoe heet u. [*what is your name*]

- **How do you say 'someone who works very hard' in English?**
  An aardvark.

- **How do you say 'I think you butcher the English language' in German?**
  Ich brauche englischsprachige Bücher. [*I need English books*]

- **How do you say 'sad fraud' in German?**
  Schadenfreude. [*merriment caused by the misery of others*]

- **How do you say 'digest' in German?**
  Zeitgeist. [*spirit of the times*]

- **How do you say 'No, I must stay' in Hindi?**
  Namaste. [*hello*]

- **How do you say 'do you know the number' in Italian?**
  Numero uno. [*first*]

- **How do you say 'sick man' in Italian?**
  Il manzo. [*beef*]

- **How do you say 'certified crazy' in Italian?**
  Certamente. [*certainly*]

- **How do you say 'My son is a psychopath' in Italian?**
  Mi sono dimenticato. [*I forgot*]

- **How do you say 'I ate llamas in the morning' in Irish?**
  Liamhás atá uaim. [*I'd like ham*]

- **How do you say 'How did you mash it?' in Japanese?**
  Hajimemashite. [*pleased to meet you*]

- **How do you say 'Oh, is she?' in Japanese?**
  Oishii. [*delicious*]

- **How do you say 'Do you see any Pakistanis?' in Latvian?**
  Cik ir pulkstenis. [*What's the time?*]

- **How do you say 'My dear Russian friends' in Russian?**

  Ну, граждане, алкоголики, тунеядцы, хулиганы...*
  (Nu, grazhdane, alkogoliki, tuneyadtsy, khuligane...)
  [*Well, citizens, alcoholics, parasites, hooligans...*]

A movie quotation that was popular all over Russia in Soviet times.

- **How do you say 'You are dead' in Spanish?**
  Adiós! [*Goodbye*]

- **How do you say 'You are super-dead' in Spanish?**
  Hasta la vista! [*till next time*]

- **How do you say 'You came for the llamas?' in Spanish?**
  ¿Cómo te llamas? [*What is your name?*]

- **How do you say 'The police are llamas too' in Spanish?**
  Llamaré a la policía. [*I will call the police*]

※ Llamas can be trained to do guard-dog duty.

Part 2 - For Fun

This part is purely for the hedonistic consumption of humour.

Financial Jokes

Some of these jokes will make sense only if you read the pink papers.

- **What is an artichoke?**
  Something that happens when you become the owner of a million-dollar painting at an auction by waving 'Hi' to a friend.

- **Truth in numbers**
  Numbers: Numbers don't lie.
  Statistics: But, we do.

- **Should you trust statistics provided by a Republican?**
  No. They tend to be conservative.

- **Why would no bank give a loan to Superman?**
  Because he has no immovable assets.

- **Why would you never get a loan from Superman?**
  Because he will see through you.

- **Why was the vampire arrested for insider trading?**
  He had inappropriate dealings with some blood bank employees.

- **Why was Count Dracula asked to take a course on moral hazard?**
  Because he wanted to invest in a blood bank.

- **How can you tell if the economy is in an inflationary spiral?**
  When the vampires start drinking each other's blood.

- **What does it mean when Count Dracula buys life insurance?**
  The tax department has picked him for a 'routine audit'.

- **Why did the cloud get a tax claim?**
  There was market speculation that it had a silver lining.

- **What did one FTSE stock say to another?**
  "Seems like you have lost a pound or two."

- **What did one startup investor say to another?**
  "What's with the pinched expression?"

- **Why did the barrel of petroleum complain to the commodity exchange board?**
  The financial papers were referring to it in crude terms.

- **Gold Investor Anthem**

  Markets boom and markets crash
  Always have some barbarous relic in your hands
  Even when your government files for bankruptcy
  Gold is nobody's liability

  Set to the tune of 'Eeny, meeny, miny, moe'.

- **Stock Investor Anthem**

  Early to invest
  Early to sell
  Ensures an investor retires in style

  Set to the tune of 'Early to bed, early to rise'.

Jokes In Advertising

These funeral parlour ads were inspired by the 1963 movie *Comedy
of Terrors* and the 1940s radio show *Duffy's Tavern* ("If you must
drink on Christmas eve, be sure to drive your car. Signed,
Cavendish, the undertaker."). Undertakers provide an under-
appreciated service to their community. If any undertaker business
wants lines for ads, they can use one of these free-of-cost on a
non-exclusive non-transferable basis. I really enjoyed writing
them. If anyone else needs advertisement lines, contact me but
you will have to donate to a charity of my choice, namely, me.

- **Funeral Parlour Ad**
  END-TIMES UNDERTAKERS: When your loved ones make their departure, we make our arrival.

- **Funeral Parlour Ad**
  CHECKER & SONS UNDERTAKERS: When loved ones check out, we check in.

- **Funeral Parlour Ad**
  ESPIRIT UNDERTAKERS: We undertake the body when they give up the ghost.

- **Funeral Parlour Ad**
  SLICK & MOB FUNERAL PARLOUR: We finish your unfinished business like nobody's business.

- **Funeral Parlour Ad**
  SPRUCE & BALM UNDERTAKERS: Some of our customers never looked better.

- **Funeral Parlour Ad**
  STORIED UNDERTAKERS: We have been in the funeral business so long that we kill the competition with our impeccable service.

- **Funeral Parlour Ad**
  HOTEL CALIFORNIA INTERNMENTS: You can check-in any time you want but you can never live.

- **Funeral Home Ad**
  PEARLY GATES PARLOUR: We will deck you up so good that your dead mother will be proud to see you arrive at the pearly gates.

- **Funeral Home Ad**
  EASY-GO UNDERTAKERS: Come hell or high water, go down there in style. Check out our luxury coffin collection.

- **Funeral Home Ad**
  KEVORKIAN UNDERTAKERS: Toughest part is taking the plunge. Come to us. Rest is easy. We will give you a harp and you will float towards heaven like an angel in no time.

- **Funeral Home Ad**
  FRANK & STEIN UNDERTAKERS: You are not taking anything to heaven with you so why bother? Hint: Organ and cadaver donation requests accepted.

- **Funeral Home Ad**
  DEADWEIGHT UNDERTAKERS: You die only once. Don't die cheaply. Check out our elite coffin collection.

- **Funeral Home Ad**
  MAIN STREET UNDERTAKERS: No money? No problem! Check out our affordable luxury coffin collection. Meet your maker in easy instalments.

- **Funeral Home Ad**
  FUNNY & DIE UNDERTAKERS: Worried your death could put a hole in your family's pocket? Perish the thought. Fun fact: Funeral coffins are not that expensive. Check out our value-for-money collection.

- **Funeral Home Ad**
  EARTHLY-WARMTH UNDERTAKERS: Choose us for the warmth of the earth.

Or, burn in hell. Hint: Cremation option available.

- **Funeral Home Ad**
EARTHLY-WARMTH UNDERTAKERS: Go six feet under. Or, sleep with fishes. Hint: Burial-at-sea option available.

- **Funeral Home Ad**
TREMBLE-GLEE UNDERTAKERS: You say good-bye first and then do business with us.

- **Funeral Parlour Ad**
DOOMSDAY UNDERTAKERS: Worried about graverobbers, vandals and the zombie apocalypse? Check out our welded-shut hermetically sealed iron casket options. Even the IRS won't be able to get in... Maybe they will but you get the idea.

- **Funeral Home Ad**
DRAKE & HULA FUNERAL PARLOUR: You are a vampire? No problem. Our Undead Coffin line models are equipped with battery-powered roller wheels (and hydraulic brakes), an oxygen tank, a digital clock (with *Tocatta and Fugue* alarm tone) and a button-operated sliding door.

- **Funeral Home Ad**
FINAL-SHOT FUNERAL HOME: Choose us. All the coolest seniors are doing it.

- **Funeral Home Ad**
BREATHE EASY UNDERTAKERS: You came to this world unprepared and crying. Leave it on your terms, with a smile.

- **Funeral Home Ad**
O'BAMUH UNDERTAKERS: Burial? We can. Cremation? Yes, we can. Turn you into ashes and shoot you into the sky or disperse over the sea?... Yes, yes, yes, we can!

- **Funeral Home Ad**
COOL-N-COZY FUNERAL HOME: Don't spend an afterlife shifting and rolling in your grave. Select a comfortable coffin today.

- **Personal Ad**
Lonely ghoul looking for a gal who is out of this world.

- **Personal Ad**
Son of the soil moleman wants to meet molewoman with down-the-earth altitude.

- **Personal Ad**
Lonely male vampire wishes to meet lonely female vampire with knockout looks, impressive teeth and shared personal taste. Call after-hours.

- **Personal Ad**
Lonely male werewolf wishes to meet lonely female werewolf. Appreciates late-night walks and moonlit dinner. Great if you can bring along a man/woman but will settle for a can of dog food.

- **Personal Ad**
Lonely male burglar wishes to meet lonely female burglar without stolen heart. Call during daytime.

- **Personal Ad**
Soft-spoken crime-fighter superhero wishes to go hang out with beautiful

superheroine with no hangups for fast cars or cool gadgets. Batgirl and cave-dwellers need not apply.

- **Personal Ad**
  Superhero more powerful than a locomotive wishes to meet beautiful superheroine with better taste in fashion. Supergirl and news reporters need not apply.

- **Personal Ad**
  Masked crusader. Lives in the jungle. Moves like a phantom. Appreciates peace and quiet. Old flames and environmentalists need need not apply.

- **Personal Ad**
  Lonely male alien seeks lonely female alien from a galaxy far far away. Should have own transport and adequate fuel supply for return trip. Age/looks no bar.

-

- **Advertising Business**
  Gotcha! We will waste valuable space like this just to prove that advertisements will attract your attention!

- **Personal Ad**
  Lonely male cat would like to meet on-the-fence female cat. Object: Unearthly late-night meowing sessions.

- **Personal Ad**
  Slightly overweight male turkey interested in taking extremely overweight female turkey to dinner. Call before Thanksgiving.

- **Personal Ad**
  Depressed feed-fed female cow would like to see pasture-raised male cow. Object: Just send your photograph in your natural surroundings. I will never leave this place alive.

- **Personal Ad**
  Lonely male dog who chewed the remote would like to meet lonely female dog in the neighbourhood. Object: Watch TV at your place.

- **Personal Ad**
  Depressed male hyena would like to meet lonely female hyena with a sense of humour. Object: Could use a few laughs.

- **Personal Ad**
  Just-released free bird wishes to meet aspiring mobster chick with clean record. Object: Escape from the man of course but no tricks.

- **Personal Ad**
  Hungry male zombie seeks lonely female zombie. Appreciates long legs and longer conversations. Strictly food for thought, not brain matter. Age/looks no bar.

- **Personal Ad**
  Lonely male dove would like to meet lonely female dove. I know a place on the father of the nation.

- **Personal Ad**
  Overweight male snake wishes to meet curvy female snake who will not recoil in horror at first meeting.

- **Personal Ad**

Me: Romantic female owl. You: Rooting-tooting male hooter. Object: Moonlit dinner. On the menu: One sumptuous snake. Two if the previous ad gets a response.

Off-The-Wall Philosophers

Are you a fan of political correctness? Do you get easily offended? Then, this section is not for you.

Vandals who deface walls should be punished. However, some of the stuff they write is so profound that it makes you pause for a while to think. These special few are born rebels, confirmed jokers or really desperate people. The jokes in this section are written along those lines but should not be construed as an excuse for vandalism.

- **ACTIONS SPEAK LOUDER THAN WORDS**
  if you are far away.

- **BEGGARS CAN'T BE CHOOSERS**
  - But they have a lot of change
  - *'Financial solicitors', not 'beggars'*
  - They chose to beg

- **A CHAIN IS ONLY AS STRONG AS WEAKEST LINK**
  So what? There will always be one.

- **THE CUSTOMER IS ALWAYS RIGHT**
  - That's why he left?
  - *Except when he wants to return stuff*

- **DANGEROUS CURVES**
  Unless you are also crooked

- **THE DARKEST HOUR IS BEFORE DAWN**
  Read *The Friday Times* instead.

Dawn (**www.dawn.com**) is Pakistan's leading English daily and was founded by the country's founder Mohammed Ali Jinnah in 1942. *The Friday Times* (**www.thefridaytimes.com**) is a weekly. It has a very funny humour section.

- **DEATH IS THE GREAT LEVELLER**
  - Taxes are the great extractor.
  - *Certainly!*

- **DESPERATE TIMES CALLS FOR DESPERATE MEASURES**
  - Poverty of ideas?
  - *Necessity is the mother of invention.*
  - New York or LA?
  - Tape or scale?

- **DIE ON YOUR FEET THAN LIVE ON YOUR KNEES**
  - Pray on your knees and fight on your feet
  - *How about I crouch a little*
  - Smoke on your lips and die on your couch
  - Drink in your hands and ~~pass out on the floor~~

- die without your liver
- **DO NOT CROSS BRIDGE UNTIL YOU COME TO IT**
  - Another one of those head-scratchers. I hate you!
  - If you cross the bridge, you fall into water.
- **DO NOT FEED THE ANIMALS**
  - You make us sick.
  - You make us fat.
- **DO NOT ~~PARK~~ IN FRONT OF GATE**
  - bark
- **DO NOT ENTER
AUTHORIZED PERSONNEL ONLY**
Really the keyhole is not big enough for anyone.
- **DO NOT LITTER**
  - ~~liter~~
  - litre
  - imperial units please
- **DO NOT SCRIBBLE**
Write legibly
- **DO NOT USE MOBILE PHONES**
  - Smash those infernal devices!
  - Is it okay to pretend? I'm going crazy here!
- **DON'T DRINK AND DRIVE**
  - Take the peanuts too
  - Pay the tab first
  - Don't forget you hat and coat
- **DON'T TAKE MORE THAN YOU GIVE**
... unless you get there first
- **DOUBT IS THE BEGINNING, NOT THE END, OF WISDOM**
I doubt it.
- **EARLY BIRD CATCHES WORM**
Come late if you have coupons.
- **EVEN A WORM WILL TURN**
  - so do not ~~crawl~~ when you can ~~walk~~
  - scrawl   talk
- **FACTS ARE STUBBORN THINGS**
  - Is this a fact?
  - I can't rub it off.

- FORGIVE AND FORGET
  - Never forget it.
  - If you just give and forget, I would like to borrow some money.

- A FRIEND IS SOMEONE WHO ~~SUPPORTS YOU WHEN YOU ARE IN THE WRONG.~~
  rescues you from the wrong

- A FRIEND IN NEED ~~IS A FRIEND INDEED~~
  may want to borrow money

- GOD CREATED MAN IN THE IMAGE OF HIMSELF
  - And God created Man's opposite, the Woman, in the image of...
  - if it's the devil, I will go to hell

- GOD HELPS THOSE WHO HELP THEMSELVES
  But thou shall not steal

- HASTE MAKES WASTE
  When you squeeze toothpaste.

- HELL HAS NO FURY THAN A WOMAN SCORNED
  Heaven has no angel than a mother to a newborn.

- I THINK. THEREFORE, I AM.
  - You are what?
  - You are definitely something.
  - i for incomplete.
  - I can't get it out of the head.
  - My eyes! I hate it when they do that!

- IDLE HANDS ARE DEVIL'S PLAYGROUND
  I was idling here. I don't know what came over me.

- IMITATION IS THE SINCEREST FORM OF FLATTERY
  Imitation is the sincerest form of flattery.

- IT IS BETTER TO GIVE THAN RECEIVE
  - if what you give is punches.
  - Hopefully, it is not a cold
  - Or the coronavirus

- IT IS BETTER TO BE POOR AND HAPPY THAN RICH AND MISERABLE
  - Of course. Ask any poor guy.
  - Or a rich one

- JESUS SAVES
  - Devil charges interest

- *Taxman collects from both*

- **KNOWLEDGE IS POWER**
  Can it light this bulb?

- **LAUGHTER IS THE BEST MEDICINE**
  Then, don't make me laugh.

- **LIVING WELL IS THE BEST REVENGE**
  Stop it. You are killing me.

- ~~**LOOK BEFORE YOU WALK**~~
  ≥ Look up from your phone, dummy. ≤

- **LOVE MAKES THE WORLD GO AROUND**
  It is all that unwanted talk that makes it spin

- **MAN CREATED GOD**
  - Try using God as a dependent on your tax returns
  - *Government created God?*

- **MONEY DOES NOT GROW ON TREES**
  Of course not. It is made from trees.

- **MISERY LOVES COMPANY**
  and pain loves incorporation.

- **NEVER JUDGE A BOOK BY ITS COVER**
  Explains why old-paper marts remove the cover when they weigh it.

- **NEVER SAY NEVER**
  - Better late than NEVER
  - *It NEVER rains but pours*
  - Lightning NEVER strikes the same place twice
  - You are never too old to learn

- **NEVER SPEAK ILL OF THE DEAD**
  But they always say what *illness* they died from

- **NO ALCOHOL**
  - Tooo late. I am already drnuk.
  - *prohibited or no stock?*

- **NO BILLS**
  What's the postman doing in the bathroom?

- **NO DOGS**
  On the menu?

- **NO HORN**
  What if it is a bullock cart?

- **NO FISHING**
  - What will sharks eat
  - Polluted or prohibited?

- **NO SOLICITATIONS**
  - We are too broke to buy anything
  - MLM salesman lives here

- **ONE GOOD TURN DESERVES ANOTHER**
  Beware of borrowers.

- **A PENNY SAVED IS A PENNY EARNED**
  Don't tell the IRS.

- **PRACTICE MAKES PERFECT**
  - perfect what?
  - Practice writing complete sentences.

- **REMAIN SILENT AND APPEAR FOOLISH THAN SPEAK AND REMOVE ALL DOUBT**
  Only practice will make you perfect.

- **QUESTION EVERYTHING**
  Who wrote this?

- **SILENCE IS GOLDEN**
  Will they buy it?

- **SLOW COWS**
  - And invisible!
  - Who can slow cows?

- **SPEAK SOFTLY AND CARRY A BIG STICK**
  - Use a cell phone for longer distances
  - Spoken like a pole vaulter

- **SPEED KILLS**
  - What do you you care?
  - They need you for the taxes
  - Speed does not kill. People kill people.
  - It's not the speed – it's the deceleration!

- **TALK IS CHEAP**
  But some expressions are priceless

- **TAKE CARE OF THE PENNIES AND THE POUNDS WILL TAKE CARE OF THEMSELVES**
  - Do not eat pennies
  - Still overweight

- Pennies? Pounds? This is Merica – U.S. of A!

- **TO ERR IS HUMAN. TO FORGIVE IS DIVINE.**
  To foment is devilish

- **TOMORROW NEVER COMES**
  - Don't hire it then
  - *Haste makes waste*

- **TRESPASSERS WILL BE SHOT**
  Take a selfie

- **THERE IS NO SUCH THING AS A FREE LUNCH**
  - Can you pay back your parents?
  - *Everything does not need to have a price tag*
  - Best things in life are free

- **TWO WRONGS DO NOT MAKE A RIGHT**
  Around a block, two lefts will.

- **UNITY IS STRENGTH**
  Too many cooks spoil the broth

- **WASH YOUR HANDS WHEN YOU LEAVE THE BATHROOM**
  - The door handle is dirtier than the toilet seat.
  - *I hate you*

- **WOMEN CAN BE JUST AS GOOD AS MEN**
  And just as mistaken.

- **YOU ARE NEVER TOO OLD TO LEARN**
  You cannot teach an old dog new tricks

- **YOU CANNOT WIN THEM ALL**
  So defeat them

Political Jokes

- **What is a politically incorrect name for a pressure cooker?**
  Whistleblower.

- **What is a politically incorrect name for stealing?**
  Quantitative easing.

- **What is a politically incorrect name for a butcher?**
  Piecemaker.

- **What is a politically incorrect name for vegetarians?**
  Plant killers.

- **What is a politically incorrect name for non-vegetarians?**
  Animal lovers.

- **What is a politically incorrect name for a designated driver?**
  Plunge-protection team.

- **What are politically incorrect names for alcohol?**
  - Toxic assets.
  - Bio-fuel.
  - Socialized Medicine.
  - Chemotherapy.

- **What are politically incorrect name for a drunk?**
  - Extrovert; free-speech activist; and non-conventional philosopher.
  - Green-fuel activist.

- **What is a politically incorrect name for a sober person?**
  - Introvert.
  - Anti-social element.
  - Loner.

- **What is a politically incorrect name for a drunk who has no idea where he is?**
  Internationalist.

- **What is a politically incorrect name for a drunk who is desperately trying to see clearly but cannot?**
  Reform-oriented.

- **What is a politically incorrect name for a drunk who is trying various ways to stand up but is unable to?**
  Technocrat.

- **What is a politically incorrect name for a drunk who thinks the world is spinning around him?**
  Revolutionary.

- **What is a politically incorrect name for a drunk who is holding his head because he thinks the world is spinning around him?**
  Counter-revolutionary.

- **What is a politically incorrect name for a drunk who has just banged his head on the lamp post?**
  Confrontationist.

- **What is a politically incorrect name for a drunk who has banged his head on**

a lamp post and is now engaged in an animated conversation with it?
Pugilist.

- **What is a politically incorrect name for a drunk who is holding on to the lamp post for dear life?**
  Protectionist.

- **What is a politically incorrect name for a drunk who climbs the lamp post and gets electrocuted?**
  Shock-therapist.

- **What is a politically incorrect name for a drunk who refuses to leave the bar?**
  Institutionalist.

- **What is a politically incorrect name for a drunk who is trapped in the revolving door?**
  Undecided.

- **What is a politically incorrect name for a drunk who is spinning inside the revolving door?**
  Centrist.

- **What is a politically incorrect name for a drunk who has passed out on the floor?**
  Unaffiliated.

- **What is a politically incorrect name for a politician who climbs the greasy pole and refuses to back down?**
  Columnist.

- **What is a politically incorrect name for a politician who climbs the greasy pole and then immediately back down under criticism?**
  Scenophobe.

- **What is a politically incorrect name for a kid who refuses to take baths?**
  Conscientious objector.

- **What is a politically incorrect name for a miser?**
  Economist.

- **What is a politically incorrect name for a plastic surgeon?**
  Feminist.

- **What did the clown say to his psychiatrist after he joined politics?**
  "I feel like I am surrounded by buffoons."

- **How did Gandhi become bald?**
  Gandhi went to the forest and did *tapas* (meditate/penance) without a break. But, even after two days, God failed to appear before him. Gandhi became very angry and broke his *tapas*. As he was just about to leave, God appeared and said "Gandhi, what do you want? Ask me anything." But, Gandhi was still angry and said "I don't need a single hair from you!"

- **TN Seshan**
  Seshan was a feared Chief Election Commisioner. He cleaned up elections in India. For the first time since Indira Gandhi's Emergency, politicians and government employees were afraid of someone. Before one election, he was

inspecting preparations in Chennai. One journalist asked him about reports that a political party (MDMK, I think) was distributing spinning tops to children to secure votes. Seshan did not say if it would be considered for disqualification but he said that it was a good thing they did not have an elephant for their party symbol.

- **What is a politically incorrect name for a kid who tries to explain his poor report card?**
  Activist.

- **What is a politically incorrect name for a parent who hides the tin with chocolates on the top shelf?**
  Elitist.

- **What is a politically incorrect name for a kid who eats the chocolates in the top shelf and then gets caught?**
  Slow, idiot or pacifist.

- **What is a politically incorrect name for a sibling who finds the chocolates in the top shelf before you can?**
  Thought criminal.

- **What is a politically incorrect name for a sibling who can reach the chocolates in the top shelf?**
  Height criminal.

- **What is a politically incorrect name for an older sibling who prevents you from reaching the chocolates in the top shelf?**
  Obstructionist.

- **What is a politically incorrect name that a parent calls you when you get caught and your story changes each time you tell it?**
  Revisionist.

- **What is a politically incorrect name for a sibling who is too chicken to get into trouble or does not get caught often enough?**
  Conformist.

- **What is a politically incorrect name for a sibling who always has a backup plan?**
  Escapologist.

- **What is a politically incorrect name for a sibling who does get caught but does not get punished as often as you do?**
  Expert.

- **What is a politically incorrect name for a sibling who manages eliminate his tracks before you bring it to your parents' attention?**
  Survivalist.

- **What is a politically incorrect name for a sibling whose problem-escaping skills have improved from pacifist to escapologist really quickly?**
  Evolutionist.

- **What is a politically incorrect name for an older sibling who steals stuff from you and gives them to his friends for free?**
  Socialist.

- **What is a politically incorrect name for an older sibling who always promises to return the stuff he has stolen from you but never does?**

Communist.

- **What is a politically incorrect name for a sibling who is too chicken to get into trouble and when you get into trouble he is there to tell you 'I told you so'?**
  Moralist.

- **What is a politically incorrect name for a sibling who comes up with a plausible excuse for any situation?**
  Innovator or child prodigy.

- **What is a politically incorrect name for a sibling who get in and out of trouble without the slightest damage whatsoever?**
  Constitutionalist.

- **What is a politically incorrect name for a sibling who backs up your version of the story?**
  Loyalist.

- **What is a politically incorrect name for a sibling who rats on you?**
  Populist.

- **What is a politically incorrect name for a sibling who rats on you and also correctly explains the motive?**
  Conspiracy theorist.

- **What is a politically incorrect name for a sibling who rats on you, explains the motive and backs it up with proof?**
  Crazy conspiracy theorist.

- **What is a politically incorrect name for a sibling who rats on you with extreme attention to detail?**
  Archeologist.

- **What is a politically incorrect name for a sibling who tells your parent the exact differences between what you promised and what you actually did?**
  Perfectionist.

- **What is a politically incorrect name for a sibling who rats on you with exaggerated detail?**
  Inflationist.

- **What is a politically incorrect name for a sibling who pokes holes in your 'cover' story?**
  Acupuncturist.

- **What is a politically incorrect name for a sibling who ratted on you and failed but made your parents not trust you anymore?**
  Controversialist.

- **What is a politically incorrect name for a sibling who threatens to rat on you but is ready to offer you a deal?**
  Mercantilist.

- **What is a politically incorrect name for a sibling who offered you a deal and then ratted on you?**
  Dichotomist.

- **What is a politically incorrect name for a sibling who does not believe in the statute of limitations and continues to extort stuff citing crimes committed long ago?**

Imperialist.

- **What is a politically incorrect name for a sibling who threatens to rat on you and refuses to cut a deal?**
  Antimaterialist.

- **What is a politically incorrect name for a sibling who does not just rat on you but also tells about your threats to use force?**
  Antimilitarist.

- **What is a politically incorrect name for a sibling who does not just rat on you but also tells about your use of force?**
  Victimologist.

- **What is a politically incorrect name for a sibling who whittles down the crime despite your best efforts to exaggerate it?**
  Abstractionist.

- **What is a politically incorrect name for an older sibling who forces you into his crime when you threaten to rat on him?**
  Neocolonialist.

- **What is a politically incorrect name for a sibling who rats on your attempts to subjugate him?**
  Abolitionist.

- **What is a politically incorrect name for a sibling who threatens to rat on another sibling who threatened to rat on you?**
  Salvationist.

- **What is a politically incorrect name for a parent who refuses to believe your spin of the story?**
  Subjectivist.

- **What is a politically incorrect name for a parent who does not want to hear your legitimate excuses?**
  Russophobe.

- **What is a politically incorrect name for a parent who refuses to believe your 'act of God' story?**
  Rationalist.

- **What is a politically incorrect name for a parent who grounds the kid and banishes him to his room?**
  Isolationist.

- **What is a politically incorrect name for a parent who remembers the exact number of times you made the same mistake before?**
  Numerologist.

- **What is a politically incorrect name for a sibling who rats on you and suggests punishment options?**
  Lobbyist.

- **What is a politically incorrect name for a sibling who takes what you have and then makes you do his errands to get it back?**
  Conservationist.

- **What is a politically incorrect name for a younger sibling who is still nibbling at the top of her chocolate bar when you have finished yours eons ago?**

Chauvinist.

- **What is a politically incorrect name for an older sibling who grabs your chocolate bar when you are still nibbling the top of it?**
  Hijacker.

- **What is a politically incorrect name for a younger sibling who is still nibbling at the top of her chocolate bar when you have finished yours eons ago and refuses to share hers with you?**
  Exclusivist.

- **What is a politically incorrect name your younger sibling calls you when you try to explain what may have happened to the remainder of the chocolate bar she placed in the chiller?**
  Fantasist.

- **What is a politically incorrect name for your older sibling who eats your chocolate bar and then begs you not to tell your parents?**
  Apologist.

- **What is a politically incorrect name for your older sibling who thinks he can get away with it?**
  Optimist.

- **What is a politically incorrect name for your younger sibling who thinks you cannot get away with it?**
  Pessimist.

- **What is a politically incorrect name for a younger sibling who takes the window seat while you bring in the luggage?**
  Opportunist.

- **What is a politically incorrect name for a younger sibling when he explains to the horrified parent how you hit him?**
  Dramatist.

- **What is a politically incorrect name for a younger sibling who walks in and ruins everything?**
  Anarchist.

- **What is a politically incorrect name for a younger sibling who walks in, ruins everything and then threatens to rat on you?**
  Terrorist.

- **What is a politically incorrect name for a younger sibling who walks in, ruins everything, threatens to rat on you and then offers to cut you a deal?**
  Humanist.

- **What is a politically incorrect name for a younger sibling who walks in, sees everything and then ignores it?**
  Solidarist.

- **What is a politically incorrect name for a younger sibling who gets everything simply by asking while you have to beg and/or scream?**
  Welfarist.

- **What is a politically incorrect name for a friend who listens to your joke and then tells others as if he invented it?**
  Plagiarist.

Rajinikanth Facts

Meteorite Incidence From 1988 to 2019

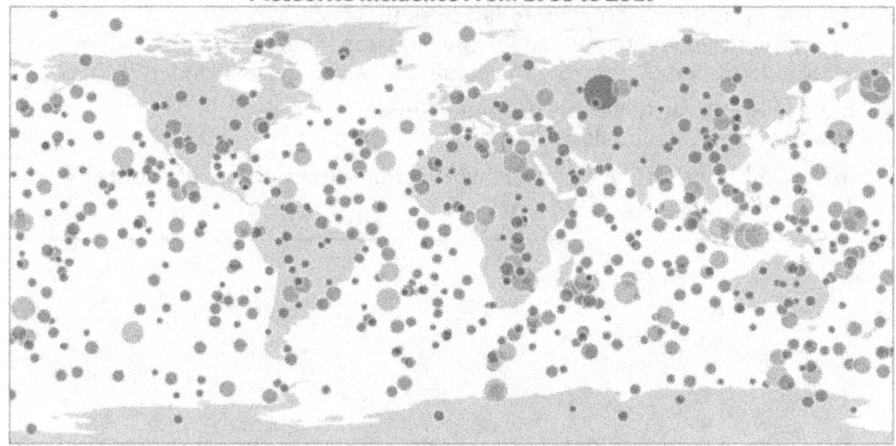

Rajinikanth lives in southern India.
Data source: NASA

America has Chuck Norris. India has Rajinikanth. Learn the facts.
DISCLAIMER: This research study was not sponsored by Microsoft.

- **What would happen if you subtract infinity from infinity?**
  Indeterminate.

- **What would happen if Rajinikanth subtracts infinity from infinity?**
  Zero.

- **What would happen if a lightning struck Rajinikanth?**
  Nothing. That's how he lights his smoke.

- **Is not smoking injurious to health?**
  To your health? Of course. It is different with Rajinikanth. Rajinikanth is injurious to smoking.

- **What would happen if a meteorite tried to strike Rajinikanth?**
  It gets classified as a meteor.

- **What would happen if a cyclone tried to strike Rajinikanth?**
  It goes into a major depression.

- **What would happen if a stray asteroid struck Rajinikanth?**
  Who knows? He might let it strike a friendship with him.

- **What would happen if a stray asteroid really struck Rajinikanth with force?**
  It would get bounced back to its belt and become known in its circle as "the one that almost got away".

- **What would happen if a tsunami struck Rajinikanth?**

It will be struck with awe and freeze.

- **Has someone written Rajinikanth's biography?**
  The Limca Book of Records was mostly about him so you could consider it as one.

- **Was Rajinikanth ever reprimanded in school?**
  Yes, many times, such as when for the question, "what do you get when you divide zero by zero", he wrote the actual answer instead of 'indeterminate'.

- **How did Rajinikanth get his driving license?**
  He made the RTO chief do an 8.

- **How did Rajinikanth become the world champion in a staring contest?**
  The statue blinked.

Chuck Norris won against the Sun.

Breakup Jokes

If this book was named '2000 ways to break up with your spouse', it would not be off the mark. I hate romantic stuff and this book is targeted at kids.

- **What did one number say to another?**
  "He seems odd."

- **What did the other number reply?**
  "Yes, he seems a bit odd."
  [It was a binary number.]

- **What did one number say to another?**
  "I think she is trying to get even."

- **Why did the two sets break up?**
  They had nothing in common.

- **What did one ultraviolet ray say to another?**
  "I don't think we are on the same wavelength."

- **What did the day planner say to the calendar?**
  "Sorry, I already have a date."

- **What did Supergirl do when Superman came home late?**
  She flew into a rage.

- **What did the male kangaroo say to the female kangaroo when he came home late?**
  "Now, honey, don't jump to conclusions."

- **Why did the applied engineering couple break up?**
  Their relationship was good on principle but bad on execution.

- **Why did the civil engineering couple break up?**
  - There was this huge wall between them.
  - The relationship had come to a full circle and they did not want to repeat it.
  - Unresolved issues were piling up and they did not know what to do.

- o   Everything came crashing down.
- **Why did the electrical engineering couple break up?**
  The spark had gone of out their relationship.
- **Why did the electronic engineering couple break up?**
  They were always short-circuiting each other.
- **Why did the mechanical engineering couple break up?**
  - o   They tried but everything came to a complete stop.
  - o   She threw a spanner in the works.
- **Why did the nanoengineering couple break up?**
  They found mistakes in the smallest of things.
- **Why did the project engineering couple break up?**
  They meant well but there were execution failures at every stage.
- **Why did the software engineering couple break up?**
  They went into an infinite loop of fighting and sulking.
- **Why did the programmer couple break up?**
  No issues.
- **Why did the systems engineering couple break up?**
  It seemed like that they had taken the only way in and if they delayed there may not be a way out.
- **Why did the structural engineering couple break up?**
  They realized that their relationship was built on a weak foundation.
- **Why did the textile engineering couple break up?**
  They wore each other's patience down to a thread.
- **How did the 3D printing couple break up?**
  He would get all bent out-of-shape over nothing.
- **Why did the absent-minded couple break up?**
  He forgot her birthday.
- **How did she know it was her birthday?**
  Yahoo Mail wished her 'Happy Birthday' when she logged in.
- **Why did the absent-minded couple make up?**
  They forgot everything.
- **Why did the accountant couple break up?**
  Marriage cost his mental peace.
- **Why did the accountant couple make up?**
  Separation cost his bank balance.
- **Why did the actor-actress couple break up?**
  - o   He was tired of her daily drama and felt upstaged by her.
  - o   He refused to stick to the script and was always acting up.
  - o   They were not entertaining any questions now.
- **Why did the actuary couple break up?**
  He was not all he was cracked up to be.
- **Why did alien couple break up?**
  - o   He was so insincere she felt like she was talking to an alien.
  - o   Although they were on the same planet, it seemed like they were light ears

away.

- **Will the alien couple make up?**
  It seems like a remote possibility.
- **Why did alien couple make up?**
  There was nobody like her in the big wide universe.
- **Why did the archeologist couple break up?**
  They were again and again fighting over issues from ages past.
- **Why did the art critic couple break up?**
  They criticised each other using utterly unintelligible sentences.
- **Why did the astronaut couple break up?**
  - Their relationship had cratered.
  - Ever since she went to space, she just was not the down-to-earth girl she once was.
  - She would speak to him only through mission control.
- **Why did the astronaut couple make up?**
  - They went over the moon.
  - He promiser her the moon.
  - They went on a second honeymoon.
  - It was written in the stars.
- **Why did the atheist couple break up?**
  - They did not believe in each other.
  - He sickened her beyond belief.
- **How did the bartender couple break up?**
  - What he brought home was peanuts.
  - He could not stay away from alcohol.
- **How did the biologist couple break up?**
  - They hated each other with every cell of their being.
  - He thought she was like a rose when they first met but now he thinks of her more in terms of stinging nettles.
- **Why did the book critic couple break up?**
  - She said his promises were empty words.
  - He remained a big mystery to her.
  - She claimed she had read him from cover to cover and there was nothing of value between them.
- **How did the book critic couple break up?**
  During the court proceedings, she threw the book at him.
- **Why did the book critic couple make up?**
  He promised to be more understanding.
- **How did the bomb-disposal squad couple break up?**
  He was totally blown away by her decision.
- **How did the botanist couple break up?**
  She felt that he was at the root of all her troubles.
- **What happened to the cannibal who fought with his wife?**
  He got roasted.
- **Why did the cannibal couple break up?**

o Each time he made a small mistake, she chewed his head off.
o When food was low, she took an unhealthy liking for him.
o They were both consumed by visceral hatred for each other.
o He got seriously burned by her.
o He asked for her hand and she refused.
o The marriage cost him an arm and a leg.
o She savagely attacked him when he revealed his political affiliation.

- **Why did the cannibal couple make up?**
  He was prepared to make any sacrifice.

- **Why did the carpenter couple break up?**
  She told him not to darken her doorway again.

- **Why did the carpenter couple make up?**
  Her door was always open for him.

- **Why did the cartoonist couple break up?**
  They had changed into caricatures of what they initially thought of each other.

- **Why did the chef couple break up?**
  o No matter how how they sliced and diced it, it did not feel right.
  o He catered to her every wish and whim, but it was never enough.

- **Why did the chef couple make up?**
  o They warmed up to each other.
  o They hashed together a compromise.

- **Why did the chauffeur couple break up?**
  o Their relationship hit a roadblock.
  o She drove him crazy.
  o He put the relationship on a permanent overdrive.
  o She got him right where he wanted.
  o She drove him to despair.

- **Why did the chiropractor couple break up?**
  o He cramped her style.
  o She restricted his freedom of movement.

- **Why did the clown couple break up?**
  o Living with him was a big joke.
  o He refused take her seriously.
  o She was tired of his silly excuses.

- **Why did the clown couple make up?**
  He mimed his way back into her heart.

- **Why did the contortionist couple break up?**
  o He was willing to bend backwards to accommodate her but she remained stiff that the relationship was permanently broken.
  o His tolerance to her antics was stretched to the limits.

- **Why did the contortionist couple make up?**
  Any reports that said they were breaking up was quite a stretch.

- **How did the coronavirus couple break up?**
  o When it came to spending money, his wallet was in a permanent lockdown.
  o They were social-distancing even before the pandemic hit.

- **How did the coronavirus couple make up?**
  They had been in love before but not with the same ~~fever~~ fervour.

- **How did the costume designer couple break up?**
  Don't worry. It was like a blessing in disguise.

- **How did the cricket batsman–batswoman couple break up?**
  - They hoped for a long innings but it is over now.
  - He ran out when he could.
  - He was tired of playing defence.

- **How did the cricket batsman–batswoman couple make up?**
  She was a quite catch.

- **How did the cricket bowler couple break up?**
  - She threw him out.
  - Maiden over.

- **How did the cricket bowler couple make up?**
  - He was always her fowl-weather friend.
  - They were ready for a second innings.

- **Why did the crossword hobbyist couple break up?**
  - He remained a puzzle to her.
  - He can take a hint when he was not wanted.
  - They accused each other of being very difficult.
  - He could not get it across to her that her attitude was going down.
  - She left him many hints but he would not catch a clue.
  - He was an annoying stickler for correctness.

- **Why did the crossword hobbyist couple make up?**
  They put their heads together and came up with the solution.

- **How did the crossword hobbyist couple make up?**
  They were lost for words.

- **Why did the DIY/maker couple break up?**
  They tried to fix the relationship themselves but realized that it was beyond repair.

- **Why did the DIY/maker couple make up?**
  - They could not stay aPART.
  - If you break it, you fix it. That was their policy.
  - They were really made for each other.
  - They had vowed to make it work.

- **Why did the electrician couple break up?**
  He said it was no fault of his that she blew her fuse every day. What exactly happened afterward is not known. Sparks flew all over the place.

- **Why did the fireman–firewoman couple break up?**
  - The fire in their relationship had died out.
  - The marriage was beyond rescue.
  - He just could not handle the pressure of being married to her.

- **How did the historian couple break up?**
  Marrying her was a monumental blunder.

- **Why did the hypnotist couple break up?**

- He was out of his mind all the time.
  - She was always under a state of delusion... pretending like she were a queen or something.
  - He was tired of her mind games - always interfering with his thought processes.

- **Why did the hypnotist couple make up?**
  He could not get her off his mind.

- **Why did illusionist couple break up?**
  When the illusion crumbled, they were not happy with the reality that remained.

- **Why did Invisible Man and Invisible Woman break up?**
  - They saw through each other and did not like it.
  - He wouldn't accept her for who she really was.
  - When he looked at her, he looked at her flaws. Not the real HER!

- **Why did the janitor couple break up?**
  - Serious problems piled up. They could not be just brushed away.
  - She would not touch him with a ten-foot pole.

- **Why did the janitor couple make up?**
  He swept her off her feet.

- **How did the jail warden couple break up?**
  - Living with her all these years was punishment enough.
  - Being married to her was like a death sentence.
  - He tried to escape many times but she always beat him into submission.

- **Why did the jeweller couple break up?**
  The relationship was fundamentally flawed.

- **Why did the jester couple break up?**
  They were at their wits' end.

- **Why did the journalist couple break up?**
  - He was the bearer of bad news.
  - "No comment!"
  - Marriage is not a democracy and freedom of speech exists only in denial.

- **Why did the judge couple break up?**
  - Whenever she wanted to talk, he asked her if the matter was scheduled for a hearing.
  - Whenever she wanted to talk and said it was important, he asked her to file a review petition.
  - She held him in utter contempt.
  - He would not abide by her rules anymore.

- **Why did the judge couple make up?**
  The matter was settled out of court.

- **How did the launderer couple break up?**
  Don't know. They didn't want to wash their dirty linen in public.

- **How did the lawyer couple break up?**
  - They acquitted themselves with much credit.
  - He summoned up the courage to say no.
  - Where there is a will, there is a way (out).

- **Why did the lawyer couple make up?**
  He rejected all charges without prejudice and she decided that reconciliation was the best course of action.

- **How did the lazy couple break up?**
  His lackadaisical attitude became his undoing.

- **Why did the lexicographer couple break up?**
  o His love had lost its meaning to her.
  o She was not careful in picking her words.
  o It was a silly misunderstanding.
  o He gave her a word of advice.

- **How did the lexicographer couple break up?**
  They hurled the choicest epithets against each other.

- **How did the lexicographer couple make up?**
  They could not describe it. Words failed them.

- **How did the lift operator couple break up?**
  He said her upper floors were empty.

- **How did the lift operator couple make up?**
  They did not want to escalate the situation.

- **Why did the minimalistic couple break up?**
  o Whatever excuses he gave, she was having none of it.
  o He did not mean much to her anymore.
  o He gave her his 100% but it still was nothing.
  o He was economical with truth.

- **Why did the minimalistic couple make up?**
  o Something is better than nothing.
  o She said he was good for nothing.
  o There is more to a marriage than a man and a woman living together. There was also this other thing called love.
  o She was worked up over nothing.

- **Why did the nurse couple break up**
  o She left him in stitches.
  o She left him in splits.
  o She lost her patience.
  o There was a limit to his patience.

- **Why did the nurse couple make up**
  He was exactly the medicine she was prescribed.

- **Why did the parliamentarian couple break up?**
  o She used unparliamentary language.
  o He could never get to be the speaker.
  o If he came late, question hour could drag on for several hours.
  o She had no confidence in him.
  o Every day, she would unload a litany of complaints about him and before he could reply to any of that, she would say, 'End of discussion!' and adjourn.

- **Why did the postal worker couple break up?**
  o He said she was bad news and she said he was a certified mental case.
  o She was like an overweight package with insufficient postage.

- His brain seems to have been put in a package and returned to sender.
  - She tried to stamp her authority and refused to address his concerns.
  - He had a hate-hate relationship with her dogs.
  - He was nothing to write home about.
- **Why did the postman couple make up?**
  He sent her a message that melted her heart and she sealed the deal.
- **Why did the police couple break up?**
  - Living with her was like institutional torture.
  - She beat him with his *lathi* when he (out of habit) demanded a bribe to do household chores.
  - When he came home late, she just lost it.
- **Why did the police couple make up?**
  He stole her heart... again.
- **Why did the physicist couple break up?**
  Things had reached a boiling point in their relationship.
- **Why did the physicist couple make up?**
  She melted on seeing drops of condensation in his eyes.
- **Why did the plumber couple break up?**
  - Suddenly, everything took a turn for worse.
  - For years, it was leaking but one day it turned into a flood.
  - Living with her left him emotionally drained.
- **Why did the plumber couple make up?**
  If she was resin, he was like the ideal bonding material.
- **Why did the printer couple break up?**
  - He did not like to stay on the margins while she took up all the space.
  - She left him in the gutter to bleed.
  - He did not want to be bound by her rules.
  - They fell out of line with each other.
- **Why did the printer couple make up?**
  - There is no need to get wrapped up over nothing.
  - They did not want to put themselves in a bind over nothing.
- **Why did the professor couple break up?**
  He was tired of listening to her lecture every day.
- **Why did the programmer couple break up?**
  They needed a break from each other. (Maybe Rachel was a programmer at heart.)
- **How did the programmer couple break up?**
  They are still processing what happened.
- **Why did the publisher couple break up?**
  - They were not on the same page on many things.
  - That chapter of their life is over.
- **Why did the psychiatrist couple break up?**
  - Attention deficit disorder.
  - Hyperactivity disorder.
  - Foot-in-the-mouth disorder.
  - Oppositional defiant disorder. [This medical term was probably coined by a

three-year-old child. It refers to opposition to 'authority figures'.]
  - She gave him a piece of her mind.

- **Why did the quiz couple break up?**
  - When asked why he was late, he never gave the correct answer.
  - Even when food was low, he always asked for a bonus round.
  - Their time was up.
  - He said something was seriously wrong with her and she said he could not be more wrong.
  - She would not give him a second chance.
  - He left her with no choice.

- **Why did the quiz couple make up?**
  - They really liked their consolation prizes and wanted a do-over.
  - They did not want to take any chances.

- **Why did the rock climber couple break up?**
  - She was condescending towards him.
  - She told him to take a hike.

- **Why did the stand-up comic couple break up?**
  - His jokes were mostly about her and she failed to see the humour in them.
  - He could not take her insults sitting down.
  - They could not stand each other.

- **Why did the speech therapist couple break up?**
  - She just would not shut up.
  - Whenever he wanted to speak, she shushed him into silence.
  - He was so terrified that whatever he wanted to say just died in his throat when he looked at her.
  - He wanted to end the many years of suffering in silence.

- **Why did the speech therapist couple make up?**
  They decided to talk things over.

- **How did the speech therapist couple make up?**
  They were speechless.

- **Why did the spelling bee couple break up?**
  They both wanted to have the last word on everything.

- **Why did the terrorist couple break up?**
  - He came home late and she just exploded.
  - Break? He totally blew it out of the sky.
  - She welcomed him with open arms.

- **Why did the tight-rope walker couple break up?**
  - He had really gone out of bounds this time.
  - She dumped him because her faith in him was shaken.
  - She could not be swayed by his honeyed words.
  - She thought she was in good hands but he let her down.
  - Famous last words: "You know what your problem is? You need to loosen up a little."
  - She was nagging him and he said, "Will you cut it out?"

- **Why did the tight-rope walker couple make up?**
  - The bonds between them just would not break.

- o He promised to do better managing his life-work balance and she was inclined to believe him.
  - o It was time to take the plunge again.

- **Why did the vampire couple break up?**
  - o He became a real pain in the neck and she began baying for his blood.
  - o He could not put food on the table.
  - o His table manners were atrocious.
  - o When she said he sucked the life blood out of her, he just smiled.
  - o It was beyond the pale of expression.
  - o He was not much of a talker. (Dead men tell no tales.)
  - o He did not know when to quit.
  - o He could not give a satisfactory explanation as to where he was going at midnight or what he was doing at that time.
  - o After feasting on an anæmic victim, he put the bite on her.
  - o She threatened to knock his teeth out and use it as a paper-punching machine.
  - o He left a bad taste in her mouth.
  - o Living with her was a constant nightmare for him.
  - o Sometimes, she scared the living daylights out of him.
  - o She was always in a comBATive mood that she gave him high blood pressure.
  - o She complained that he would often give her low blood pressure.
  - o He was a shadow of his former self.
  - o It was clear as day to her that he was emotionally a dead man.
  - o Her batty disposition was a sad reflection on her part.
  - o Just after she got her hair a nice perm, he frightened her and straightened it all out.
  - o They were facing an existential crisis but he was more interested in rolling out impressive party tricks.
  - o He told her she was getting long in the tooth.
  - o He took an eternity to take decisions.
  - o He always said he was buried in work.
  - o This relationship was past its expiry date.
  - o She would pretend to be catatonic if he asked her to help with housework.
  - o He did not want to be caught dead with her.

- **Why did the vampire couple make up?**
  - o He was very good at flying to the ceiling and cleaning those hard-to-reach places. Very useful when you live in a castle.
  - o He was low maintenance and always… always appreciated her 'good' looks.
  - o She was a hæmophiliac and seeing him always made her blood freeze… clot immediately.
  - o He was good at disposing door-to-door salesman and tax collectors.
  - o He was very good at removing bottle caps and opening tinned food.
  - o He does not hog the remote during the day.
  - o He was a good listener. There is something to be said for men who do not talk back.
  - o His smile always excited her.
  - o He said he will always be there for her.
  - o They did not want their past cast a shadow on their future.
  - o Before he realized he was neck-deep in trouble, she made a sucker out of

him.
  - Their love lasted hundreds of years yet they felt like it had just begun.
  - Dental insurance is cheaper under the family plan.
  - It was too early to write the epitaph on this relationship.
  - He promised to be very much alive to her discomforts.
- **Why did the werewolf couple break up?**
  What he brought home was just dog food!
- **Why did the teacher couple break up?**
  - She wanted him to be quiet and raise his hand if he wanted to say something.
  - She made him stand up on the bench if he did anything wrong.
  - She would not let him inside the house when he came late without a note from his father.
  - She blamed her but he felt he was the wronged person.
  - She wanted to teach him a lesson.
- **Why did the English teacher couple break up?**
  She would not take 'No' for an answer. She wants an explanation in 100 words or more.
- **Why did the English teacher couple make up?**
  - He cast a spell on her.
  - She forgave him after he wrote a 1000-word essay, to her satisfaction, on how much she meant to him.
- **How did the maths teacher couple break up?**
  - They had irreconcilable differences.
  - They did not know the answers to many of their problems.
  - She could not count on him for anything good.
- **Why did the physics teacher couple break up?**
  There was no chemistry between them.
- **Why did the chemistry teacher couple break up?**
  - It was an overreaction.
  - Their feud reached a boiling point.
- **Why did the biology teacher couple break up?**
  They magnified each other's faults under a microscope.
- **How did the history teacher couple break up?**
  They wanted to forget the past.
- **How did the geography teacher couple break up?**
  They were poles apart.
- **Why did the kindergarten teacher couple break up?**
  She got angry for no rhyme or reason.
- **Why did the sports teacher couple break up?**
  They decided to quit playing games and called it a day.

Books By V. Subhash

I invite you to visit my site **WWW.VSUBHASH.IN**, and check out my other books, special discounts, sample PDFs and full ebooks. In 2020, I started publishing books. For two decades before that, I have been publishing feature articles, free ebooks (old editions still available), software (server/desktop/mobile), reviews (books, films, music and travel), funny memes and cartoons. You can follow these adventures on my blog: **http://www.vsubhash.in/blogs/blog/index.html**

My books for children are under the pseudonym **Ólafía L. Óla** (because it has laugh and LOL).

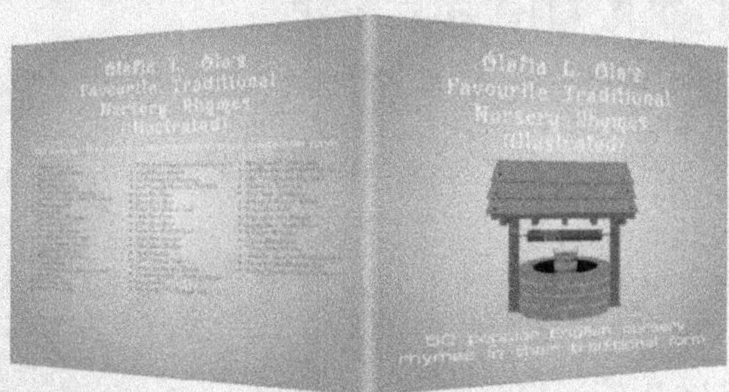
Gladis L. Gist
Favourite Traditional
Nursery Rhymes
(Illustrated)
50 popular English nursery
rhymes in their traditional form

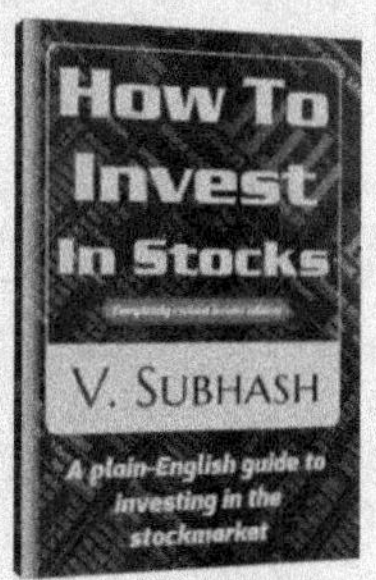
How To
Invest
In Stocks
Completely revised fourth edition
V. SUBHASH
A plain-English guide to
investing in the
stockmarket

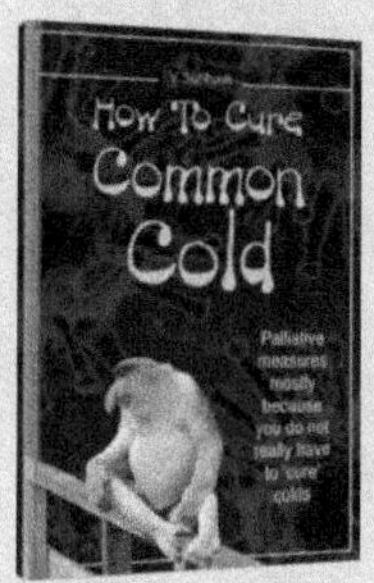
V. Subhash
How To Cure
Common
Cold
Palliative
measures
mostly
because
you do not
really have
to 'cure'
cold

V. Subhash's
Email
Newsletter
Strategies
For Profit

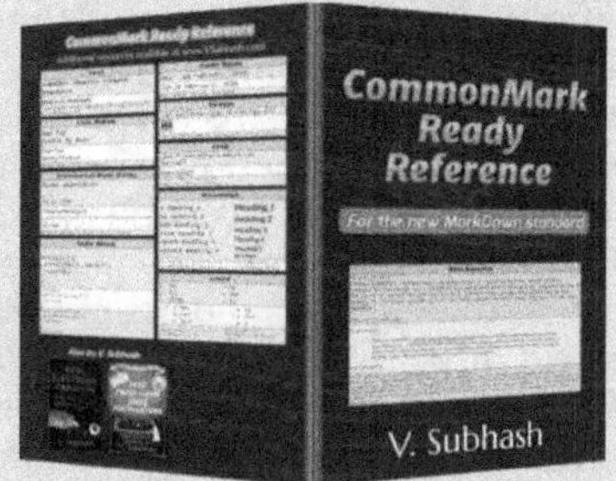
CommonMark
Ready
Reference
For the new MarkDown standard
V. Subhash

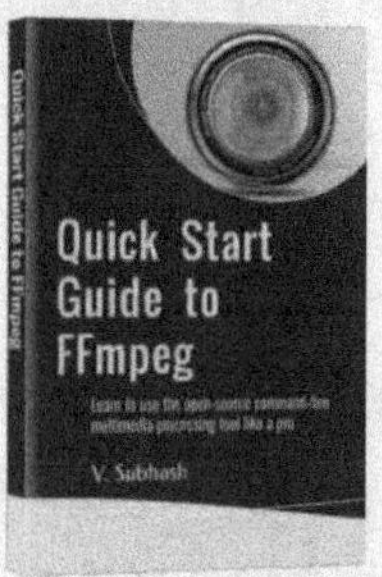
Quick Start Guide to FFmpeg
Quick Start
Guide to
FFmpeg
Learn to use the open-source command-line
multimedia processing tool like a pro
V. Subhash

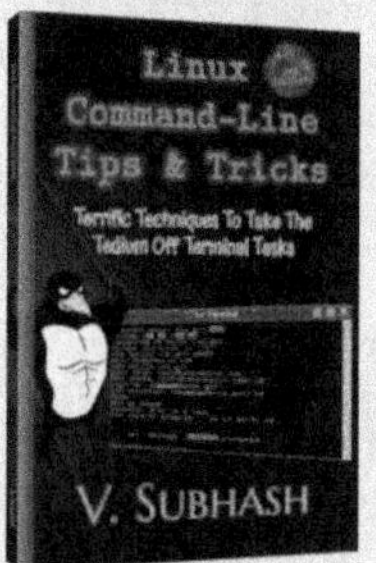
Linux
Command-Line
Tips & Tricks
Terrific Techniques To Take The
Tedium Off Terminal Tasks
V. SUBHASH

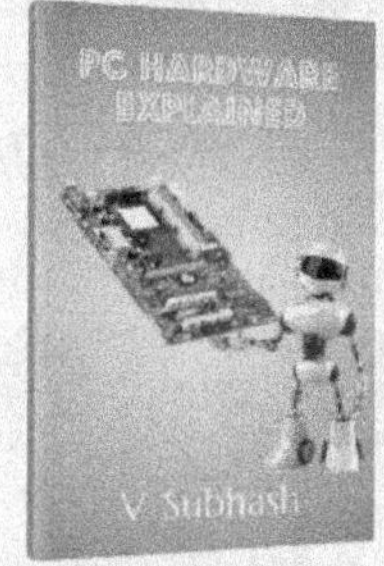
PC HARDWARE
EXPLAINED
V. Subhash

COOL
ELECTRONIC
PROJECTS
Simple • Low-cost • Cute • DIY
Naughty • Practical • Fun
V. SUBHASH

HOW TO INSTALL SOLAR
HOW TO
INSTALL
SOLAR
V. Subhash

THE
DEVIL'S
DICTIONARY

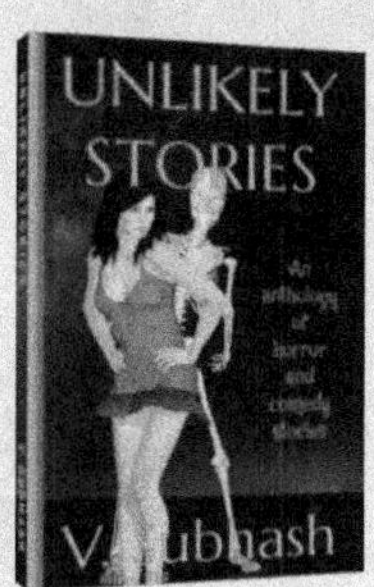
UNLIKELY
STORIES
An
anthology
of
horror
and
comedy
stories
V. Subhash

About the author

V. Subhash is an invisible Indian writer, programmer and cartoonist. In 2020, he published one of the biggest jokebooks of all time and then followed it up with a tech book on FFmpeg and a 400-page volume of 149 political cartoons. Although he had published a few ebooks as early as 2003, Subhash did not publish books in the traditional sense until 2020. For over two decades, Subhash had used his website **www.VSubhash.com** as the main outlet for his writing. During this time, he had accumulated a lot of published and unpublished material. This content and the automated book-production process that he had developed helped him publish 21 books in his first year. In February 2023, Apress (SpringerNature) published his rewritten and updated FFmpeg book as *QUICK START GUIDE TO FFMPEG*. Thus, by early 2023, Subhash had published 30 books! In 2022, Subhash ran out of non-fiction material and tried his hand at fiction. The result was *UNLIKELY STORIES*, a collection of horror and comedy short stories. After publishing its second edition in 2023, Subhash has decided to pause his writing. Subhash continues to pursue his numerous other hobbies and interests, several of which have become the subject of his books such as *COOL ELECTRONIC PROJECTS*, *HOW TO INSTALL SOLAR* and *HOW TO INVEST IN STOCKS*. He was inspired to write his gigantic jokebook after years of listening to vintage American radio shows such as *Fibber & Molly* and *Duffy's Tavern*.

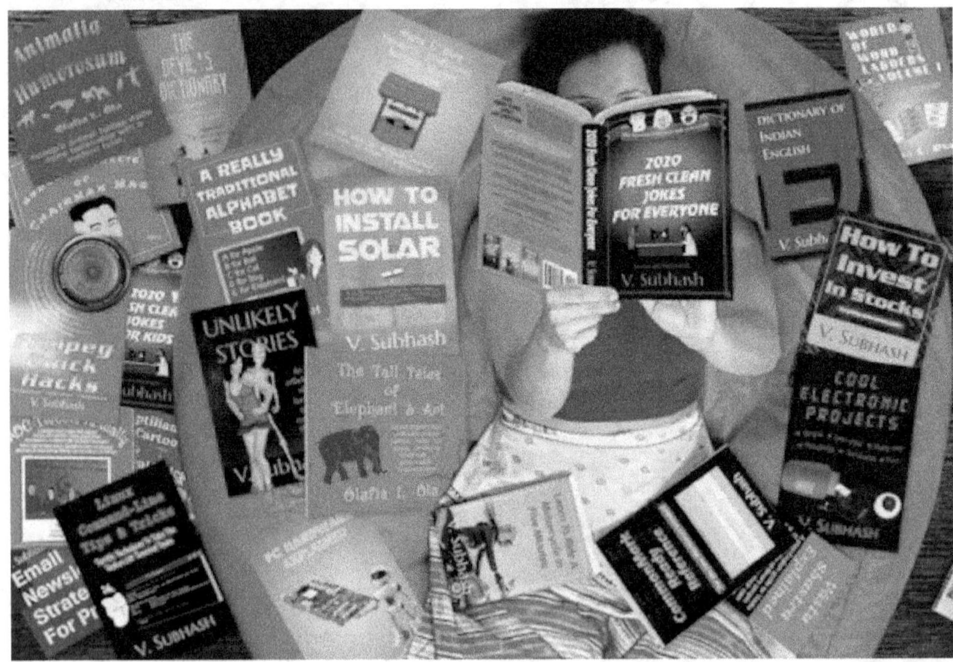